After less than two minutes, everyone realized the newspaper office was beyond saving.

"Oh, my God!" Harry Andrews gasped as he came to a breathless halt beside Steele. "The bastards have burned me out."

"You been told lots of times, Harry," Boxer growled as he joined the small group out front of the saloon. "That building's been a fire risk ever since you set up shop."

"Go to hell, Boxer!" the newspaperman snarled. "Newsprint just burns! It doesn't explode!"

At that moment a woman screamed and went on screaming for a long time, until all other sounds except those of the dying fire were silenced. She was holding something in both hands, staring down at it with wide eyes set in a face totally devoid of color. The woman gasped, and had time to hurl the object away from her before collapsing in a faint. Everyone could now see it was a high-sided riding boot. With a severed leg still in it, three inches of charred, bleeding flesh protruding through the top . . .

85¢

THE ADAM STEELE SERIES:

No. 19
George G. Gilman

ADAM STEELE

THE TARNISHED STAR

PINNACLE BOOKS   NEW YORK

ADAM STEELE #19: THE TARNISHED STAR

Copyright © 1981 by George G. Gilman

An original Pinnacle Books edition, published by special arrangement with New English Library, Ltd.

First printing, July 1981

ISBN: 0-523-41452-8

Cover illustration by Fred Love

Printed in the United States of America

PINNACLE BOOKS, INC.
1430 Broadway
New York, New York 10018

For Mike Stotter—
who stepped into the breach.

THE TARNISHED STAR

CHAPTER ONE

Sun City looked like a good place to live in. Which, Adam Steele thought as he surveyed the town through the shimmering heat haze of Southern California, probably made it a bad town to die in. But he heeled his gray gelding forward anyway, tugging on the reins to steer the horse across the rock-littered slope and onto the trail which ran into town.

Despite the blistering midmorning heat, the Virginian wore a pair of black buckskin gloves: these gloves which contoured every bump and hollow of his hands were the reason he thought about dying. For Steele, who was a practical materialist in all other respects, had one idiosyncrasy: whenever he sensed danger was threatening him, he pulled on the scuffed and stained gloves. It was a habit he had picked up during the War Between the States: a habit which the events of the long violent peace had not allowed him to

1

lose. For he considered the pair of gloves a lucky charm, as important to his survival as his constant alertness and his skills with weapons.

He did not look like a man of violence as he reached the trail and allowed his mount a free rein, heading down into the town on the Pacific shore. He was small of stature, standing just a fraction above five feet six inches, and compactly built. He had a long and lean face with regular features arranged in a pattern that gave him a brand of nondescript handsomeness: the eyes coal black and the mouthline gentle, set into flesh that was scored with furrows and stained dark brown by exposure to the elements. At first glance he looked older than his true mid-thirties age, for his once red hair was prematurely gray.

He wore a tailored gray suit with blue stitching at the seams, a purple vest and a white shirt which was trimmed with lace. There was a gray, low-crowned Stetson on his head and brown and white riding boots on his feet. A gray silk kerchief hung around his neck, unknotted. His entire dudish outfit was marked by the signs of a rough passage along more than one trail.

Beads of sweat coursed across his dust-layered cheeks and soaked into the bristles of a three-day beard. And he became self-consciously aware of his disheveled and dirty appearance as the open trail from the south broadened into the neat and clean main street of Sun City.

The ocean was out of sight now, behind the high cliffs in back of the sand dunes and the salty tang of coastal air was also missing: masked by

2

the stronger, citric smell which infiltrated the town from the orange groves to the north and east.

Close up, Sun City looked as attractive as it had from the top of the rise.

"Howdy."

"Good mornin' to you."

"Welcome to Sun City, stranger."

An old man sitting in a rocker chair out front of the blacksmith shop was the first to greet Steele. Then, further down the street, toward where a cross street formed a broad intersection, two women called out to him as they emerged from a dry goods store. Other people on the street or sidewalks nodded or smiled to him.

Steele inclined his head in response to the men and raised a gloved hand to touch the brim of his hat whenever a woman greeted him, becoming increasingly aware of the dirt ingrained in his flesh and coating his clothing as he saw that the citizens of Sun City were as neat and clean as their town.

The intersection of Main and Pacific Streets was the commerical center of the community and Steele angled his horse across to the north-east corner where the Sun City Hotel stood, a two-storey red-brick building with signs at each side of the entrance listing all the creature comforts a respectable traveler might require: Rooms, Meals, Hot Baths, Saloon, Livery Service.

Even as he reined the gelding to a halt by the vacant hitching rail and started to swing down from the saddle, Steele was treated to an example

3

of the hotel's efficiency. For a tall and skinny boy of about sixteen with a face plagued by boils stepped out over the threshold between the fastened open double doors.

"Take care of your horse, sir?" he asked, smiling broadly. "Feed and water him if you're just passin' through. Board and curry him if you intend stayin' on awhile."

"Feed and water for now," Steele answered, his Virginian origins sounding strongly in his voice as he drew his rifle from the boot hung forward of the saddle. "Grateful to you, son. I'll let you know if there'll be anything else."

"You're welcome, sir," the boy said as he stepped down off the sidewalk and took up the reins of the travel weary gelding. He led the animal around the corner onto Pacific Street and then into an alley that gave onto the rear of the hotel.

"If you're huntin', mister, it better just be animal type game."

Steele had his back to the hotel entrance as he scanned the four stretches of street leading off the intersection. He spotted the barber shop, on the north section of Main, just as the man with a gravel voice spoke the warning.

He turned and saw the sheriff of Sun City eyeing him critically. A man who was six feet tall and broadly built—his bulk solid looking except around his belly where the excess flesh drooped over his gunbelt. He had a square, florid face dominated by narrow blue eyes. Because of his complexion, his thin lips were almost invisible.

4

His mildly menacing expression had a fixed quality about it, as if he viewed every aspect of his life in the same manner. He was about forty-five.

The badge of his office was pinned to the breast pocket of his black shirt. His pants, boots and hat were also black. His belt was tooled leather with a fancy buckle, the holster worn high on the right hip and holding a Frontier Colt with polished wood grips on the butt.

"Looking for a place to clean up and rest is all," Steele answered.

The lawman nodded, his expression unchanged. "Just ask at the desk, mister. You could have left your rifle with your horse. Young Dwight ain't the kind that steals things."

It had been many years since Steele had carried a handgun. Ever since he had first learned how to shoot on his father's plantation back in Virginia he had preferred a rifle to a revolver. The plantation no longer existed, its fields overgrown and the big house a blackened, burned-out ruin. The man who had owned it was buried under the weeds close to the house: his only bequest to his son the rifle which was now canted casually to Adam Steele's left shoulder. A .44 calibre five-shot Colt Hartford with a cylinder and hammer action. A weapon developed during the Civil War and later used mostly in gun sports.

The model which the sheriff of Sun City resented was distinctive in two respects. Its rosewood stock was scorched black in places by the fire which destroyed the Steele house and, screwed to one side of it, was a gold plate inscribed with the legend: *To Benjamin P. Steele, with gratitude—Abraham Lincoln.*

"Never crossed my mind he was," the Virginian answered. "Just that wherever I go, so does the rifle."

The red-faced lawman nodded again and moved out of the shade of the doorway and onto the sun bright sidewalk. "Guess most folks got fixed ideas about some things, mister. Like me, I don't never trust a man who wears gloves when the weather ain't cold. That always seems gunfighter style to me. Nothin' personal, so long as you stay outta trouble."

He stepped down off the sidewalk and ambled lazily across to his office which was on the south side of the western stretch of Pacific Street.

"Don't pay no mind to Jack Boxer, sir," a woman advised. "Keeping the peace is the easiest job there is in Sun City. Talking tough to strangers is about the only effort he gets to make to earn his pay."

She was in her early twenties, blonde haired and beautiful. Short and slender with delicate features and a girlish figure. Her smile showed perfect teeth and put a sparkle in her light gray eyes. There was a rhinestone studded ring on the third finger of her left hand. She wore a workaday white dress that displayed her figure without emphasizing it too much. Her petticoats rustled as she turned and glided across the lobby and behind the desk.

Glad about that, ma'am," Steele said as he trailed her as far as the patrons' side of the desk and scattered dust on the carpet when he took off his hat. "Just hope I don't cause him to exercise any more of his authority."

He glanced around the lobby, which had white-washed walls hung with prints, half a dozen armchairs set on the floor, a stairway leading to the upper storey and three doors in addition to the main entrance. One was marked SALOON, another RESTAURANT and the third PRIVATE. The furnishing and decor were serviceable rather than plush, the place suggesting that its owner had visited a first class big city hotel and attempted to create a similar atmosphere on a limited budget.

"You'll be staying with us, sir?" the woman asked.

Steele nodded.

She stooped and lifted the register out from under the desk. "For how long?"

"Long as it takes, ma'am."

She seemed on the point of asking him to explain the comment, her smile replaced by a frown.

"Sorry," Steele told her, showing a boyish smile that took away the years which his gray hair added to his age. "For as long as my stake can stand the rate."

As he used the pen from the ink stand to sign the register, the girl frowned at the top of his head, not convinced that he was telling the truth. But the smile was back on her face when he looked up and she handed him a key.

"Room five . . ." She turned the register to read his name. " . . . Mr. Steele. One dollar a night. Breakfast is twenty-five cents and a bath is five cents. Fifty cents a day for the livery, plus feed."

"In advance?"

"That won't be necessary."

"I'd like a hot bath, ma'am."

"I'll have Dwight see to it as soon as he is through attending to your horse. Third door on the right from the top of the stairs. Dwight will show you where to go when the bath is ready."

"Grateful to you."

"You're welcome."

As he climbed the stairs, went through a doorless archway at the top and found his room, the Virginian knew the woman was lying. Maybe her initial welcome to him had been genuine, but then he had allowed his guard to slip when he had told her "Long as it takes." Something must have shown on his face as he spoke these words—something which warned her Sheriff Jack Boxer was right to be suspicious of the stranger.

The room was functional, containing a bed, a closet, a dresser and a strip of carpet. There was a window hung with net and drape curtains which provided a view across the intersection. The mattress on the bed was thinly stuffed, but comfortable enough he discovered when he lay on it. He gazed up at the ceiling and thought, indirectly, about death again. Because he was considering the reactions of the only two people in Sun City who had got close enough to him to gain more than a first impression of the stranger. Close enough to see that Adam Steele was no ordinary saddletramp heading away from somewhere and toward anywhere.

He had never set out to be a trouble maker. In fact, until the outbreak of the War Between the States he had lived a privileged and trouble-free life, fortunate to be born the son of one of Virginia's wealthiest plantation owners.

In the war he had fought for the Confederacy, riding as a lieutenant in a cavalry troop. Violence and death had exploded about him then and he had acquitted himself well, using his hunting and killing skills—acquired for sport—to fight the Unionist enemy. And, while most of his comrades fought for a just cause, he had an additional spur to his driving ambition for victory: the fact that his father supported the north.

But then the long and bloody war was over and, amid the euphoria of peace, the Steele father and son were willing and anxious for a reconciliation. Which was not to be; for on the night Abraham Lincoln was assassinated, Ben Steele also died. Lynched in the barroom where he was due to meet his son for the first time in more than five years.

On that misty April night Adam Steele fired the first shot in the violent peace as he set out to track down and take his revenge on the men who hanged his father. That was the only time in his life when he had set out purposefully to kill for entirely personal reasons. And he had done this impulsively, recklessly, slaughtering the innocent as well as the guitly in his half-crazed desire for vengeance.

Fate had punished him for his crimes—far more severely than the law ever could. For one of those he killed was a deputy sheriff who was also his oldest friend. But fate had never considered that the mental suffering this brought about was sufficient. And, ever since Jim Bishop's corpse had tumbled from the saddle, Adam Steele had been compeled to ride with violence trailing him or lying in wait for him. From New Orleans to the West Coast, from the Mexican border lands to Oregon, the Virginian had drifted, eking out a living and always close to dying.

And a man could not live so long on the knife-edge of violent death without the experience stamping signs upon his face. In the eyes and the set of the mouth. The lawman had seen these signs, and so had the woman. Both were aware that the stranger in town meant trouble.

Yet how could they know he was not looking for it? That it was merely his pre-ordained destiny that trouble should explode around him, inevitably drawing him into its vortex like some helpless twig forced into the center of a whirlpool.

"Tub's ready, Mr. Steele," the youngster yelled as he rapped a fist on the door of room five. "Down at the end of the hall. Everythin' you need's in there."

The Virginian rose from the bed with a sigh, replacing his frown with a smile of relish. There had been no element of self-pity in his mind as he reflected upon the kind of life he led. It was the only one open to him, as he had proved more than once when he had tried to alter it. So now he was resigned to accepting what he was and to enjoying the few luxuries that came his way—like a clean bed in a neat hotel room and a tub of hot water to soak in. People's reactions to him? As the son of a rich man with all the privileges this entailed during his formulative years, the views of him held by others had never been of any consequence.

He left his hat in the room but carried the Colt Hartford with him. The tub was in a windowless room and Dwight had lit a lamp so there was light after Steele had closed and locked the door. He stripped naked and soaped himself all over before lowering himself into the tub so that only his head was above the surface of the soon dirty water. He soaked himself for a full thirty minutes before he stepped out and toweled himself dry. Then, with distaste, put on again the clothes which were stiff with old sweat and stained by dirt.

Fresh clothes had become virtually an unattainable luxury of late, for Steele had finally learned to get his priorities right—to spend what little money came his way on the necessities of life. But old habits died hard and so it was that, as a Virginian gentleman fallen upon hard times, he was never able to rid himself of a feeling of self-disgust whenever his appearance fell short of his surroundings.

When he was fully dressed, he bent his right leg which caused a split in the outside seam of his pants to gape: thus he was able to push a throwing knife into the opening and nestle it in his boot sheath.

He left the bathroom then, and paused only to collect his hat before he descended the stairway into the lobby. The woman was still behind the desk, but was seated on a stool now, working on some needlepoint. She heard his footfalls and looked up, smiling.

"If you'd like a drink, Mr. Steele, I'll be pleased to open up the saloon."

"No thanks, ma'am. I lost my taste for alcohol a long time ago."

That had been in a cantina of a village over the border in Mexico. When he had drunk himself into a nightly stupor for a long time, trying to drown his remorse over the murder of Jim Bishop.

"My name is Helen Stewart. Sun City is a friendly place. Most folks call each other by their first names. The restaurant won't be open until lunch time. But I'll be pleased to put a coffee pot on the stove."

The Virginian was again suspicious of her friendly attitude. She was making too much effort to establish a relationship with a guest at the hotel, and he was certain it was not for the obvious reason.

"Maybe later, Miss Stewart," he replied as he crossed to the sun-bright doorway and ran the back of a gloved hand over the bristles on his jaw. "Reckon the inner man can wait until the outer one is respectable."

"Well, anything you want, you just let me

know," she called after him as he stepped out onto the sidewalk.

Sweat began to ooze from his pores again the moment he was in the direct glare of the sun which was inching across a cloudless sky toward its midday peak. And his underwear was sticking to his flesh by the time he reached Sam's Barbering Parlor. Sun City seemed to be the kind of town where the pace of life was never fast and in the mounting heat of a morning drawing to a close there was hardly any activity at all.

Main Street was deserted, the women having completed their shopping. Storekeepers stayed deep in the shade of their premises. There was a low-keyed murmuring of talk beyond the batwing doors of the Lucky Lady Saloon, next door to the barber shop. And the clack of type being set in the office of the *Sun City News*, which was diagonally opposite the door through which Steele went. The tinkling of a bell at the top of the frame roused the short, fat barber from his slumbers in the parlor's only chair.

"Howdy, mister!" he greeted enthusiastically, brushing off the chair as if he felt he may have contaminated it. "Shave, cut, hot towels, friction— you name it, Sam'll supply it."

"Shave and cut, feller," the Virginian drawled, dropping into the chair and resting his rifle against his leg. It was pleasantly cool in the parlor and the white cover the barber draped over him was crisp and clean.

"You like to talk, listen or neither, mister?"

"I get the choice?"

13

"Sure, mister. Sun City's a friendly town. Folks here like to welcome strangers. Strangers are customers and customers are always right. You just say what you want."

"Told you. Shave and cut."

Steele saw the reflection of Sam's round and fleshy face in the mirror and caught the brief flicker of dislike which showed between the ending of the smile and the start of a neutral expression. Then the man got to work, silently and efficiently. While Steele relaxed, enjoying another small but infrequent luxury.

When the job was complete and the cover was removed, Sam accepted the quarter payment with a nod, then pointed at the Colt Hartford.

"Sheriff John Boxer won't like to see you carryin' that rifle around, mister."

"He already made that known, feller," Steele answered.

"Oh."

"Yes. We reached an understanding."

"Good."

The Virginian stepped out of the parlor and his nostrils caught the scents of boiling coffee and frying food amid the pervading citric smell from the orange groves. His stomach protested mildly that it had been a long time since breakfast.

He started across the street.

"You bastard, I'll kill you!"

The words reached out into the sunlight over the top of the Lucky Lady's batwing doors. Shrieked by a man gripped by a degree of anger that sent his voice to an almost soprano pitch.

"Don't!" somebody else yelled, the single word vibrant with horror.

The shot was awesomely loud, amplified within the confines of the saloon to the volume of a canon's roar. But, even as he hurled himself to the rock-hard, dust-layered street, Steele knew what had caused the explosion. The twin hammers of a double-barrelled shotgun falling in unison against two charges.

A spray of crimson droplets intermingled with black pellets gushed out over the top of the batwings. Then the doors crashed open and a man staggered out. Dead, but with his shocked nervous system still working his muscles. He got as far as the edge of the sidewalk before gravity took control, dragging the corpse down in a slow, corkscrewing action.

Steele saw this along the top of the Colt Hartford's dully gleaming barrel: for he had instinctively taken aim and cocked the hammer as soon as he hit the street.

The dead man no longer had a face, just a red, highly sheened pulp, smaller in area but displaying much the same gory, formless design as the bloody tissue and sinews which the blast had revealed across his chest. The man came to rest on his back so that the blood, seeking the lowest level, drained away to show the shattered bones of the cheeks, the jaw and the rib cage.

The batwing doors flapped once more and were still.

"Jesus Christ, Rich!" a man croaked in the

15

saloon. "You didn't have to give him both barrels!"

"County pays the freight," came the laconic response. "One shell extra won't put up taxes."

The lethargy of Sun City was abruptly gone. Footfalls pounded on the sidewalks and street and men and women shouted questions. As Steele rose to his feet and eased the hammer back to the rest, a man skidded to a halt beside him and demanded:

"Who is it?" Then he gave a choked cry and gasped, "Oh, my God, it's Carl Parton."

"Don't know the name, feller," Steele drawled as he canted the Colt Hartford to his shoulder and eyed the shattered and bloodied corpse impassively. "Even if I did, I couldn't put a face to it."

CHAPTER TWO

"You did it, Doonon!" the man beside the Virginian snarled as another man showed his head and shouldered above the tops of the unmoving batwing doors. "You killed Carl!"

The doors were flung open by being hit with something hard. Doonon stepped out on to the sidewalk and everyone on the street saw it was the muzzles of the shotgun which had hit the doors, as the barrels were snapped closed with new charges in the breeches.

Doonon, who was a giant of a man, held the shotgun angled across his broad chest as he raked his dark eyes over the faces of the gathering crowd. But swung it down to hold it leveled, one handed, when he spotted the man who had shouted at him. When he had done this, the deputy's badge showed up clearly against the black fabric of his shirt.

"Sure enough did, Mr. Andrews," the lawman admitted nonchalantly. "For resistin' arrest. And that better be what you print in your newspaper."

Rich Doonon was about thirty. Six and a half feet tall and weighing more than two hundred and twenty pounds. The way his black shirt and blue pants contoured his flesh warned that little of his bulk was made up of excess fat. He had a handsome face with bronzed, crinkled skin. His hair was yellow and hung long and unkempt to his shoulders. In addition to his shotgun, he carried a matched pair of Remington revolvers in low slung holsters. His clothing was clean and freshly pressed and his guns were well cared for.

"I'll print the damn truth!" Andrews retorted, his temper still high but showing no fear of the shotgun which covered him. To either side of him everyone edged away, except Adam Steele, who glanced incuriously at the newspaperman.

Andrews was the same age as Doonon but had been cast in an entirely different mould. His build was rangy and he had a smooth-skinned face with a pale complexion. His hair was black and neatly trimmed and his gray eyes had a look of weakness in them. But there was a determination in the set of his mouth and cut of his jaw. Without the rich growing moustache he would have looked much younger. He was dressed in baggy pants, a crumpled shirt and a bootlace tie which he had unknotted. His appearance was of the appealing, little-boy-lost kind rather than handsome.

"You won't print nothin' until I've had an official report from my deputy, Harry!" Sheriff Boxer snapped as he elbowed his way through the crowd to the front and then glanced briefly at the shattered corpse before staring long and hard at the Virginian.

"You have anythin' to do with this, mister?" he demanded.

Steele reflected momentarily upon abstract thoughts of the violence which inevitably exploded when he was least expecting it. Neither the thoughts nor his action in dismissing them altered the lines of his neutral expression.

"No, Sheriff." He nodded to the corpse. "Your deputy made that mess all by himself."

"Parton was stirrin' up trouble again, John," Doonon supplied, after staring at Steele—not quite sure if the Virginian was needling him or not. "You know the way."

"Save it, Rich!" Boxer cut in, and raised his voice. "You folks that saw it, come on down to my office! Rest of you people go about your business. If Charlie Bennett ain't here, somebody go get him and tell him there's undertakin' business to be done."

The crowd began to disperse at once, either glad to turn their backs upon the gruesome corpse or feeling a compulsion to obey the order of the lawman. Steele was among those who moved away.

Harry Andrews stood his ground. "You going to allow the press to attend, Boxer?" he demanded.

"Law business until it's cleared up and squared away, Harry," the sheriff answered. "You stop by the office later and I'll give you a statement."

Andrews muttered something under his breath,

19

spun on his heels and strode angrily back toward his newspaper office. But then his attention was captured by somebody at the intersection and he altered course again: arrived at the entrance of the Sun City Hotel at the same time as Steele. The beautiful Helen Stewart and the boil-plagued Dwight stood on the sidewalk, the woman anxious and the boy curious.

"Has it started, Harry?" Helen asked. "Is it happening, just as you said it would?"

"Was it Uncle Carl that Doonon shot, sir?" Dwight asked.

Steele went directly into the lobby, suspicious yet again of the motives of the gray-eyed blonde. For she had spoken too loudly and had divided her attention between the newspaperman and the Virginian. He sensed her eyes on his back as he angled across the lobby toward the door marked RESTAURANT, which was now standing open.

"Yes to both questions," Andrews said.

"Sonofa . . ." Dwight started. Then: "Sorry Miss Stewart. Mr. Andrews."

"That's all right, son," the newspaperman assured. "I feel like using language a whole lot stronger than that when I write about what's happening in this town."

"Come in, Harry," the woman urged. "Buy me lunch. You can't do anything until Boxer and Doonon have worked out their excuses."

Steele did not hear Andrews' reply, for he had gone through the doorway and into the small, neat restaurant with its dozen tables covered with checkered cloths. But he heard the couple come in as he sat down at a table near the window and watched a pretty Mexican girl of about fourteen approach him.

"*Señor*?" She held a pencil poised over a sheaf of papers.

Steele glanced at the menu and ordered steak with a side salad and a cup of coffee. By the time the girl had taken down his order and started back for the kitchen, Helen Stewart had selected a table and allowed Andrews to seat her. It was next to the one Steele was using but he had his back to them.

"Do you think Carter ordered it, darling?" Helen asked as the Virginian pulled off his gloves and pushed them into a side pocket of his suit jacket. Since he had left the corpse-littered Circle Bee spread many miles to the south of Sun City, he had taken to wearing the gloves at all times except when he was eating or cleaning up. A material sign that he had finally surrendered to the inevitable.

"Richard Doonon never so much as wipes his nose unless somebody tells him to do it, Ellie," the newspaperman replied and there was a heavy weariness in his voice.

"What will happen now?"

"Probably nothing, if the killing does what it's supposed to do."

"Frighten people? Are you afraid, Harry?" There was the creak of her chair and rustle of her dress fabric as she leaned across the table. Perhaps to take his hand. "I'm sorry, darling. Of course you aren't. But you . . ."

21

"I'm tired, Ellie," he replied softly. "Physically beat and tired of beating my head against a wall."

Steele gazed out through the window at the deserted intersection in the center of a town that was not what it seemed, aware that he was expected to eavesdrop. The Mexican girl delivered his order.

"Ham on rye and coffee, Maria," Helen called.

"Just coffee," Andrews muttered disinterestedly.

"You're not going to eat, darling?"

"I couldn't. I've never before seen a man with no face and his heart hanging out of his chest."

There was a pause, although the woman uttered no sound of shock. And when she did speak her voice was evenly pitched. "Neither has Franklin Carter, I bet. He hires men to do his dirty work."

Steele chewed his steak rhythmically, occasionally spearing a piece of salad with his fork, washing down the food with coffee.

"My weapons are words, Ellie, you know that!" Andrews came back sharply. "Printed words. If we resorted to the same tactics as Carter, we'd be no better than he is."

Another pause, filled only by the sounds of Steele eating. Then a flatbed wagon rolled across the intersection, heading from north to south along Main Street. A short and fat middle-aged man had control of the two horse team. On the side of the wagon was a sign proclaiming: CHARLES BENNETT—SUN CITY FUNERALS. The woman was also seated in a position to

22

see the remains of Carl Parton being discreetly transported to the undertaking parlor.

"Words are no protection against a shotgun, Harry," she warned ominously as Maria brought sandwiches and coffee to the table.

"The ideas the words project aren't for protection, Ellie!" Andrews replied hastily and the legs of his chair scraped on the floor as he stood up. "They are the only moral way to attack Carter."

Coins rattled on the table top and Andrews' footfalls sounded on the floor.

"What about your coffee?"

"I don't want it, Ellie. I have to think and I always do that best when I'm on my own."

Both Steele and the woman looked out of the window. But Andrews did not pass to go in the direction of his newspaper office.

"He's crazy, Mr. Steele," Helen said. "And he's going to be killed. I know it."

Her tone was melancholy and when Steele turned away from his empty plate to look at her he saw tears poised in the corners of her gray eyes.

"Everyone has to die some time," the Virginian told her. "I reckon it must be easier if you know you're dying for something you believe in."

He placed a dollar bill on the table top, in payment for an eighty-five-cent meal. Then put on his hat and gloves.

The woman turned sideways on her chair. "You don't have many more of those left, do you?"

"What?"

"Dollars."

"Don't worry, Miss Stewart. When I'm no longer good for the room rent, I'll leave."

"Why should I worry? I only work here. And you must know I wasn't thinking about that. Because you heard what Harry and I were talking about."

"Reckoned I was supposed to. There was no way I couldn't."

He gripped the Colt Hartford around the frame and made to stand up. But she laid a hand on his arm. And continued to keep it there until she had risen from her table and swung around to sit at his.

"You are a gunfighter, aren't you? As Jack Boxer guessed you were?"

Her beautiful face, totally devoid of make-up, showed no flaw in the bright sunlight shafting through the restaurant window. It was set in an earnest expression.

"I use my rifle when I have to," he replied, regretting that her hand was no longer on his arm: conscious of a warm sensation at the pit of his stomach as he gazed at her face and smelt the trace of some subtle perfume she was wearing.

She gave a curt nod of satisfaction, then took a deep breath and started to speak. Softly and slowly, confident that her mere presence as an attractive woman would hold him in his seat for as long as she wanted it.

"Franklin Carter is a rancher who works a big spread north of Sun City, Mr. Steele. He's rich, but greedy to be richer. And he's vain. He wants to be famous—to have his name live on long after he's dead. The way he wants to do that is to build a city. A bigger and better city than San Francisco. A New York of the West."

"Plenty of room for one," Steele put in when the woman paused to reach across to the other table and get her coffee.

"Certainly there is. Carter has the choice of almost the whole coastline of California. But his mind is set on this particular area."

"Grateful that you've told me, Miss Stewart. Some of the worst things that happened to me happened in cities. I'll make a point of riding wide if I ever come through this way again."

She gave another of her curt nods. And this time showed a brief, tight smile. "If you feel that way, you can understand why others share your opinion, Mr. Steele. Sun City is a nice little town, plenty big enough for the people who decided to settle here. It's neat and clean and full of friendly people who make honest and adequate livings. It has no crime or vice and its citizens are proud of it. You're an intelligent man. You must have seen this?"

"Heard one man threaten to kill another. Then saw him get blasted into eternity."

Helen sipped some coffee as Steele spoke, then sighed as he finished. "I was speaking in the present tense, wasn't I? As if the clock had been turned back and it was a year ago. Well, things have been changing. Twelve months or so ago a group of strangers came to town. Businessmen, engineers, geologists and construction people.

25

They spent a whole week here at Carter's expense, studying the terrain and the shoreline. Nobody would say what they were doing, but Harry worked it out. And he printed the story in the *News*. The experts were surveying this area to see if it would make a good site for a city and port. And the money men were here to consider investing in the project."

She was warming to her subject, speaking faster. But abruptly she sealed her lips and glared angrily out through the window. Steele turned his head in time to see Boxer and Doonon finish crossing the intersection and go from sight on the sidewalk out front of the hotel entrance. Then the footfalls of the sheriff and his deputy rapped against the floor of the lobby.

The Virginian and the woman looked toward the restaurant doorway as the two lawmen came to a halt on the threshold.

"Harry not here, Helen?" the red-faced Boxer asked, taking off his hat.

"He couldn't face food after seeing what that oaf did to Carl Parton," she snapped.

The sheriff's narrow blue eyes showed a momentary expression of pain. Seeing this, Steele was struck by the thought that the lawman felt something for Helen Stewart, resented the situation and events which caused her to be scornfully angry toward him.

Doonon's big hands tightened their grip on the shotgun slanted across his chest, but he displayed no other reaction to her insult.

Boxer cleared his throat. "Be obliged if you'd

give your fiancé a message, Helen. Carl Parton was drunk in the Lucky Lady. He was talkin' wild and the bartender asked my deputy to throw him out of the saloon. When Rich tried to do that peaceable, Parton threatened to kill him and went for his gun. He was so drunk there's no tellin' who he might have hit if he'd got to fire the gun. So Rich was protecting innocent bystanders as much as himself when he killed Parton. There are six witnesses to what happened and if Harry wants their names, I'll give them to him. He can talk to them. Same as to me and Rich Doonon if he wants."

He made to turn around and his deputy imitated him.

"Carl's so-called wild talk was about Franklin Carter, I bet!" the woman flung across the room.

Maria started out of the kitchen, heard the angry words and quickly withdrew through the doorway.

Boxer halted, half turned away, his hat already back on his head. "I didn't get into that, Helen. Just wanted to be sure my deputy hadn't acted outside his line of duty. Like I told you, Harry's welcome to talk with the witnesses. Guess they'll be able to fill him in."

"With any lies that suits them and Carter!"

The sheriff's face spread with a deeper than usual shade of red as he struggled to contain his own anger. He did not quite succeed. "If Andrews gets told lies and prints them, that'll be a match for a whole lot of other garbage he's published in the *News,* Helen!"

27

He completed his turn then and his steps as he left the hotel were much heavier than when he had entered. For some reason, Richard Doonon felt the need to grin broadly as he trailed the sheriff.

"Did you hear that sanctimonious claptrap?" Helen snorted after she had watched the two lawmen halfway across the intersection then screwed her eyes shut—wearing an expression that suggested she was trying to will them off the face of the earth.

"Heard Boxer tell it how it may have happened," Steele answered, and got to his feet just as the woman snapped open her eyes.

She frowned and at first the expression conveyed fear that he was leaving. But quickly she flared with anger. "Carl Parton owned the strip of cliff-top land that runs a mile north and a half mile south of Sun City, Mr. Steele! He used to run sheep on it until six weeks ago. Until one morning he found all his stock dead in the surf. All his money was tied up in those sheep and ever since he lost them Carter has been pressing to buy his land off him!"

Steele had started to move away from the table.

"Well, isn't it obvious?" she yelled after him. "Carter's cement and stone city can't be built unless it has ocean frontage for a port. And Carl's pasture is right where the port is planned to be! Carter fixed for the sheep to be tossed in the sea, and he fixed for poor Carl to be murdered!"

The Virginian halted in the doorway of the

28

restaurant but did not look back over his shoulder. "If it's as clear cut as that, it's obvious, Miss Stewart," he allowed evenly. "What's equally obvious to me is that only the people of this town have the right to stand in Franklin Carter's way if they don't like what he's doing. I'm just a stranger passing through. So it's none of my business."

"Then I misjudged you!" she countered, and moderated her tone. "I thought that trouble was your business."

Now he did look back at her, more beautiful than ever with the sun floodlighting her poignantly sad features. "No, ma'am. Staying alive is the only business I have. So I try to steer clear of trouble. On account that it could bankrupt me."

CHAPTER THREE

Steele slept throughout the afternoon and evening, sprawled fully clothed on the bed in his room with his hat over his face and his left hand fisted around the frame of the Colt Hartford. When he first went to his room after lunch it had not been with the intention of sleeping. Instead, he had meant to think over what Helen Stewart had told him and to consider whether he was interested in finding out more about Franklin Carter's grandiose plans to build a genuine city upon the site of Sun City.

But the effects of the meal combined with the dry heat of the day acted to make his eyelids heavy. And as soon as his eyes were closed, the weariness of long days in the saddle and short nights in his bedroll dulled his mind and nudged him into sleep.

When he woke up and moved his hat off his face the room was fuggy with his breathing and filled with the soft, silver light of the moon. The town was as peaceful as when he went to sleep and when he looked down from the window the intersection and streets showed empty. There were lights shining from the public rooms of the hotel below him, and from the windows of the law office, the Lucky Lady Saloon and a few other buildings. But for the most part Sun City was locked up and dark.

Not until he started down the stairs did he hear the murmuring of voices and the sounds of eating and drinking from the restaurant and barroom. He felt no pang of disappointment when he saw that an old man wearing eyeglasses had replaced Helen Stewart behind the desk in the lobby.

"I guess you gotta be Mr. Steele," the old-timer said dully, then forced a grin to his lips as he added: "Evenin' to you. I'm Myron Goldstein. Work the hotel nights for Mr. Carter. Anythin' you want, you just let me know."

"Franklin Carter owns this place?" the Virginian asked.

"This and the Lucky Lady both. Four of the town's stores as well. That of interest to you, Mr. Steele?"

He became anxious while he waited for the answer, then his lens-magnified eyes dulled again when the Virginian said:

"Just making conversation with a lonely old man, feller."

He went through into the restaurant, where four tables were occupied: three by couples with a married look about them and one by three men who had the appearance of storekeepers. The Virginian's entrance interrupted the talk, but it quickly began again and as he sat at a table he sensed nothing more than mild and natural curiosity among the diners.

"Just coffee," he told Maria, who smiled brightly at him. Then treated him to a similar expression when she brought his order.

He sipped the strong, dark brew and enjoyed the way it dissipated the stale taste of sleep from his mouth.

Dwight, his boils looking angrier and more painful under the artificial light of the ceiling-hung kerosene lamps, drew scant attention as he came into the restaurant. Until he approached Steele's table and stooped his lanky frame to speak softly.

"A message from Miss Stewart, sir. She's havin' dinner at Mr. Andrews' house. That's the last one on the east side of South Main. Said you'd be most welcome to join them if you've a mind."

This said, he turned and hurried out of the restaurant. The level of conversation rose to normal and now Steele became aware that the other people were pointedly not looking at him. He finished his coffee, left the price on the table and went out into the lobby, sensing anxious eyes like a palpable force pressing against his back.

Goldstein and Dwight were in earnest conversation behind the desk, but the boy curtailed what he was saying the moment he saw the Virginian.

"Grateful to you for bringing the message,

son," Steele said. "But I don't reckon it would be polite for me to interrupt a quiet dinner for two."

"Just told you what she told me to," Dwight responded, disgruntled. Then added: "Sir."

Steele had to open one of the double doors to step out onto the sidewalk. The night air which curled in over the high ground from the ocean was pleasantly cool and its saline smell was stronger, almost winning out on that from the orange groves.

As he started across the intersection, his destination the light-spilling batwing doors of the Lucky Lady Saloon, his mind was as clear as the air which surrounded him. For the decision was already made, even though he had spent hardly any time at all in considering Helen Stewart's implied proposition. He had awakened with his mind made up and the subtle atmosphere of expectation and anxiety he had detected in the restaurant and lobby of the Sun City Hotel had served to strengthen his resolve.

There were other people, in addition to Helen and Dwight, who were looking for a more direct and positive brand of leadership than Harry Andrews was able to give through his newspaper. And Steele's need of money more or less compelled him to offer his services. But before he did this it was important to assess the potential of the opposition.

Which was why he pushed open the batwings of the Lucky Lady and stepped over the threshold without hesitation.

33

The place was small enough to be crowded by the dozen or so patrons who stood at the bar or sat at tables, drinking, playing cards or doing both. It was a square room with the bar running all the way along the rear wall. Light was provided by lamps on each of the six round tables and showed that the saloon operated with the very minimum of creature comforts and that those who ran and used the place had little regard for cleanliness.

Only the watery-eyed and toothless bartender interrupted what he was doing to pay attention to his new customer as the Virginian moved between the tables to find a clear space at the bar. Everyone else in the smoke-filled, sweat- and liquor-smelling saloon ignored the newcomer. To the extent that Steele felt his approach had been seen and all discussion about him had ceased before he entered.

"Get you somethin'?" the broad-shouldered, big-bellied, sixty-year-old bartender asked, his voice as surly as his lumpy face.

"Beer," Steele told the man and to his own ears the single word had a strangely alien sound.

"Sure."

The Virginian read the tariff pinned to a shelf, placed the required five cents on the bar top and turned his back on the sullen-faced man as the money was taken and the overflowing glass was set down.

The customers of the Lucky Lady were all men in an age group from twenty-five to forty. Hard looking men with a day's bristles and dirt on their faces. Dressed in work clothes—three looking like ranch hands and the rest having the appearance of farmers or maybe orange growers. Only the ranch hands wore gunbelts with Colt revolvers in the holsters. There was too much talk for Steele to pick up a distinct impression of what any group was discussing. But there was certainly no laughter and no face showed a smile.

"Seems Sun City friendliness stops outside your doors, feller," the Virginian said as he turned to the bar and found the man who had served him eyeing him as sullenly as before.

The man folded his arms. "You asked for a beer and you got it, mister. You want everyone to shake you by the hand and pat your back as well?"

"Stranger causin' you trouble, Lester?" one of the men with a gun called down from the far end of the bar. He was about twenty-five with a lot of old scars on his face—from an accident or a fight.

"We're talkin' is all, Pat," the bartender growled. "And I had enough trouble in my place for one day."

"Well, if you . . ."

Pat's offer was cut short by a violent explosion—the blast setting the batwing doors to flapping and smashing one of the saloon's two windows.

"Sonofabitch!" somebody yelled as the smokey atmosphere of the Lucky Lady swirled, lamps flickered and the stench of burnt powder overlaid every other smell in the place.

"What the frig?"

"Jesus!"

Every eye was drawn to the shattered window, beyond which a multi-colored glow could be seen—light from fiercely burning flames which shone much brighter than that of the moon.

It took no more than two seconds for the men to recover from the shock of the explosion. Then they joined Steele in making for the still flapping batwings, jostling him and each other to get out on to the street and stare wide-eyed at the fire which roared and flared amid the rubble of the shattered *Sun City News* office.

Along the length of Main Street doors and windows were flung open as people rushed to see the result of this new act of violence in their town. A crowd gathered on the intersection quickly swelled, the first arrivals joined by new-comers hurrying along Pacific Street.

"Get buckets! Bring water!"

These shouted words, rising above the pande-monium of shocked questions, triggered the citizens of Sun City to positive action. People ran into and out the back of their houses, to reappear with slopping pails of water. The owner of the hardware store opened his premises to loan out more buckets. Men ran toward the blazing news-paper office while women held on to excited chil-dren or carried the protesting youngsters back to bed.

Steele remained where he was in front of the Lucky Lady Saloon while the men who had fol-lowed him out advanced on the fire. They did not help on the human chain that was formed to convey water from out back of the town livery to the front of the newspaper office, but it would have made no difference if they had. For the flames had a strong hold on the frame building and its largely timber and paper contents. And the heat of their fierce burning prevented the firefighters from getting closer than the center of the street. Thrown from such a distance, the little water that reached the target was instantly vaporized into steam.

After less than two minutes, everyone realized the newspaper office was beyond saving and the water was hurled at the house to one side and the feed and grain store on the other: to put out dangerous sparks the moment they settled on roofs and walls.

"Oh, my God!" Harry Andrews gasped as he came to a breathless halt beside Steele. "The bastards have burned me out."

The Virginian had not heard his running footfalls above the roar of the flames, the crash of falling timbers and the shouts of the firefighters. When he turned toward Andrews, he saw Helen was still running, left trailing by her fiancé. Behind her, the tall Sheriff Boxer and his towering deputy ambled along Main Street like two men heading for a Sunday afternoon picnic they knew they would not enjoy.

"Oh, my darling!" Helen choked out as tears coursed down her face which was glowing red from the exertion of her run. She gripped his upper arm with both hands.

But he didn't seem to be aware of her—his eyes

37

staring fixedly at the rapidly disintegrating building. He was standing high on his toes to see over the heads of those fighting the fire and those who merely stood and watched.

"You been told lots of times, Harry," Boxer growled as he and Doonon joined the small group out front of the Lucky Lady Saloon. "That buildin' been a fire risk ever since you set up shop in it."

"Go to hell, Boxer!" the newspaperman snarled. "Newsprint just burns! It doesn't explode!"

He stared for a moment into the sheriff's puzzled face, then swung an arm in an arc to point out the many windows of surrounding buildings which had been shattered by blast.

"Sure went up with one hell of a bang, Jack," Doonon allowed as he shifted his shotgun from across his chest to cant it to his shoulder, in the same manner as Steele.

"Okay, okay!" Boxer growled. "Maybe it was oil or ink or somethin' like that went up. I'll investigate, Harry. Should be all burned out come mornin'. I'll check over what's left soon as the heat's cooled."

"You stay away from my place!" Andrews ordered. "I don't want you poking around and destroying . . ."

"Harry!" Helen cut in when she saw the lawman's face begin to take on the deeper red of rising anger. "Remember how you ran the *News*— no accusations until the proof is certain."

A woman screamed and went on screaming for

a long time, until all other sounds except those of the dying fire were silenced. Then, by accident or design, she curtailed the high-pitch noise the moment that every eye located her. Standing in the center of Main Street at the point where it ran between the last two buildings of town and became the open trail to the north. She was holding something in both hands, staring down at it with wide eyes set in a face totally devoid of color.

"What is it, Jack?" Rich Doonon asked evenly.

The woman gasped, and had time to hurl the object away from her before her eyes went to the tops of the sockets and she collapsed into a faint. She threw it far enough to reach into a broad patch of flickering light from the flames. So that everyone could see it was a high-sided riding boot. With a severed leg still in it, three inches of charred, bleeding flesh protruding through the top.

Gasps and choked utterances of shock sounded among the watchers as the gruesome object was recognized.

"It seems that somebody's man stood a little too close to the fire," Harry Andrews muttered sardonically.

"And got more than his fingers burned," Steele added in the same tone.

CHAPTER FOUR

Boxer and Doonon waited until the danger of the fire spreading was over, then dismissed the people who had fought it. And began to search for the owner of the dismembered leg by the light of the moon and the flickering glow of the dying flames.

Despite the sheriff's disgruntled demand that it was law business, Andrews joined the search, while Helen remained beside Steele, moving closer to the blackened shell of the newspaper office as the heat diminished.

"It proves one thing, doesn't it," the woman said after a lengthy silence during which she and other curious bystanders—watching from a greater distance—had listened for a shout to tell them that the body, or another part of the body, had been discovered.

"What's that?" the Virgnian answered.

"That they were starting to be worried by what Harry wrote in the *News*."

She had dried her tears but the tracks of them still showed on the merest touch of make-up she was wearing. Her blue dress, only slightly more stylish than the one she wore during the day, was spotted with flecks of soot from the fire.

"Who exactly are *they*, Miss Stewart?"

She snapped her head around sharply to look at his profile. "You really want to know?" She was trying to mask her excitement. "When you didn't come to Harry's house, I thought . . ."

"There's Carter and Boxer and his deputy. And most of the men who drink in the Lucky Lady, I reckon. How many others?"

His soft spoken words acted to calm her and her own voice became matter-of-fact. "All the men on the town council. And Carter's hands are ready to do what he tells them. Some of the storekeepers."

"How many?"

She shrugged. "About thirty or forty, I guess. A dozen or so with a vested interest because they can see a big profit if we became a big city. The rest of them thinking the way they do because their living depends upon doing what their bosses tell them."

"How much?"

"What?"

"Boxer, come over here!" Harry Andrews yelled from the alley between the newspaper office and the feed and grain store.

The two lawmen ran around from the other side of the smouldering building, Doonon carrying the booted leg in a sack.

41

"Ellie, you don't want to look at this!" the newspaperman called as Steele and the woman moved into the mouth of the alley.

Doonon halted and turned to bar the way. Helen Stewart stopped, but the Virginian continued to advance.

"Like Jack said, mister! This is law business!" His dark eyes glittered and his voice was harsh. A sneer of contempt twisted his mouthline as he gazed down from his great height at the much shorter Steele.

"He's with us, Harry!" Helen called.

"Figured he would be," Boxer growled. "Let him through, Rich. I figure dead people ain't nothin' new to him."

"You'll regret it, punk," Doonon rasped, then swung around and led the way into the alley.

Andrews was standing by a window in the fire-blackened side wall of the building. The glass had been blasted out of the frame so it was easy for Boxer to swing a leg over the sill and step into the charred rubble. Smoke and sparks rose from beneath his feet as he moved toward something sprawled across the twisted wreckage of a flat-bed printing press. The roof of the building had either been blasted off or had fallen in to feed the flames. So moonlight shafted down to provide illumination as Sheriff Boxer went onto his haunches beside the ruined press.

"It's a body?" Andrews asked.

"Sure enough smells like roasted meat," Doonon muttered, speaking what Steele thought as he detected a familiar trace of cloying sweetness amid the more acrid taints rising from the rubble.

"With one leg missing below the knee," the sheriff confirmed, using his kerchief for a mask over his lower face as he picked up a length of charred timber to move the humped form.

"The man who did it," Andrews rasped through teeth clenched in anger.

"We don't know that," Doonon countered.

"So why the hell is he inside, you dumb . . ."

"Cut it out the both of you!" Boxer snarled. "Rich, go get Charlie Bennett."

The big deputy glared at Andrews, but then swung around to hurry away to do the sheriff's bidding. He still carried the sack containing the dismembered leg.

"Who is he?" the newspaperman asked.

"Hell, he's mangled up a whole lot more than Carl Parton was. There's no way I can . . . Wait a minute. Yeah, Harry, I know who he is."

He tossed the piece of timber away and stooped lower over the blasted and burned corpse. Then stood, turned and came back out through glassless window. His right hand was clenched into a fist, which he did not open until he had led the way out of the alley to where Helen Stewart stood. On his palm was a ring—a circle of gold with a black stone set in a claw.

"Bart Dixon," Andrews rasped.

"Ain't never seen a ring like that on anyone else's finger," Boxer allowed. "Just to be sure I'll check the livery to see if that white stallion of his is there."

The lawman seemed relieved to have a ready excuse to move away from the group. Andrews was on the point of calling after him, but again Helen clasped his arm with two hands and this time he was conscious of her grip.

"What's the use, darling?" she asked. Then, to Steele: "Dixon was foreman out at Carter's Pacific Ranch."

"Carter picked the right man for the job," Andrews murmured miserably.

"Reckon Doxon doesn't think so any more," the Virginian said evenly.

Dixon was a natural-born troublemaker," Helen said quickly, speaking to Steele as she steered Andrews into a turn and the three of them started along the street. "He got drunk almost every time he came to town and when he was drunk he started fights. The *News* was always carrying stores about how it was always the other men involved who finished up in gaol for the night. Bart Dixon threatened to fix Harry and his newspaper on several occasions."

Andrews pulled his arm clear of the woman's grip but continued to walk slowly along Main Street. Most of the bystanders had gone home. Those who remained looked at the newspaperman with expressions which spanned the lower spectrum of feelings from dejection to pity. Andrews was aware of this and his face showed a look of helplessness until the trio was across the intersection and on the empty south stretch of Main Street.

Then he displayed the determination that was

evident in his mouth and jawline. "I'm not out of the newspaper business yet, Steele! And even if I was, I wouldn't resort to the methods of men like you. I'm sorry if Ellie gave you a wrong impression, but if you're looking for work with that rifle, you came to the wrong people in this town."

He lengthened his stride and quickened his gait, to move out ahead of the Virginian and the woman. Just as Charlie Bennett's wagon pulled out of an alley beside the undertaking parlor, with the mortician holding the reins and Rich Doonon sitting on the seat beside him.

Helen stopped and Steele came to a halt beside her. There was a look of deep anxiety on the woman's beautiful face. "Please don't take any notice of him, Adam," she pleaded, using his first name easily, and touched his forearm for part of a second. "I'll make him see it's the only way. Will you wait at the hotel until I can do that?"

"How much?"

She chewed on her lower lip and he guessed she was holding back anger at his mercenary attitude. She contained it well. "Nobody has much money in this town, because it's not the kind of place where people get rich. They work hard enough to make a living and save for a rainy day. I don't know . . ."

"Thirty or forty people on one side, Miss Stewart," he cut in. "A lot of them living out on Carter's ranch, I reckon. How many against them?"

"People prepared to fight? Dwight Tuxon, a handful of old timers and . . . me."

Andrews had reached the front of his unimpressive, neglected house and was gazing back toward Steele and his fiancée. There was a kind of tense anger in his stance.

"I meant how many people are against the principle of what Carter wants to do to Sun City," the Virginian corrected.

She was aware of Andrews watching her and pointedly turned her back to him. "Everyone else in town, I think. But they're simple country folk, Adam. The kind that Harry can sway with his newspaper. But who can be frightened by Carter's tactics. They aren't fighters."

"A hundred? Two hundred?"

"Somewhere between the two. Closer to two hundred."

Steele nodded and started to swing away. "The weather could take a turn for the worse, Miss Stewart. Five dollars apiece from their rainy day money and we could be in business."

She made a sound deep in her throat, but without seeing her face he was unable to determine what emotion she was expressing. And she did not augment it with words as he strolled away from her. When he reached the front of the hotel he looked back along Main Street in time to see Harry Andrews usher the woman into his house.

He stood in the cool night air, smelling again of the ocean and the orange groves now that the fire was out, and watched Charlie Bennett's wagon start away from in front of the destroyed building. The undertaker was alone on the seat. Behind the slow moving vehicle, Doonon and the sheriff stood on the street, talking. Then Boxer left the bigger man, to go into the Lucky Lady Saloon. Doonon moved closer to the burned out office of the *Sun City News*, obviously assigned to guarding the charred rubble. After the undertaker's wagon had rolled by and into the alley beside the funeral parlor, the town became mournfully silent.

Until the hoofbeats of a slow moving horse sounded out on the north trail, disturbing the Virginian's cool and collected thoughts about his decision to involve himself with the trouble of Sun City.

He looked along the length of Main Street, seeking the source of the sound, and saw the single horse and rider in dark silhouette against the moonlight-whitened trail that came down into town from over a grassy rise. Because of the stillness of the night, the sound of the animal's easy paced approach traveled more than half a mile ahead of it.

Doonon had lit and was smoking a cigarette as he also watched the lone rider approach. But then something in the appearance of the newcomer startled the towering deputy. He dropped the half-smoked cigarette, ground out its fire under a heel and backed into the alley between the remains of the newspaper office and the feed and grain store. The shotgun which he had canted to his shoulder while he smoked was suddenly gripped in the familiar way, slantwise across his chest, just before he ducked out of sight.

The rider had closed to within two hundred yards of the north end of Main Street when

Doonon made his abrupt move. Which still meant he was over a quarter of a mile from where Steele stood in the pool of lamp light from the glass panels of the hotel's entrance doors. And even over such a distance the Virginian was able to spot the distinguishing feature of the man which had probably been recognized by Rich Doonon. For although the rider was still no more than a dark silhouette against the sloping trail, the strange attachments to his hat could be picked out. It was a conventional Stetson, but hanging down at intervals around the brim were cords with small circular items tied to them, swinging as he rode on a level with the tip of his nose and lobes of his ears. Corks, Steele guessed, for he had seen two or three men wearing such hats before—the attachments designed to keep flying insects off the face.

The rider rained his mount to a halt on the very edge of town and his head moved from side to side, as if he suspected he might not be welcome and was trying to pinpoint the position from which the trouble would explode. Whether he saw or sensed the man who was watching him from cover, when the rider heeled his horse forward he had his right hand resting on the butt of a holstered revolver.

Steele knew his own presence in front of the hotel had been noticed and noted.

"Grace, you bastard!" Rich Doonon yelled as he stepped out of the alley and into the moonlight of the street, the double-barrelled shotgun aimed from the hip.

The newcomer showed he shared a skill with Steele: in that he had not only sensed danger, but had correctly judged the direction from which it threatened. Thus, his head had swung toward the alley mouth before Doonon shouted the first word. But, the Virginian realized, the man was much quicker on the draw than he was. For the revolver was out of the holster, cocked and aimed across the front of his body before the deputy had completed the insult. And the trigger was squeezed before Doonon's hand received the message from his brain.

The man's aim was as skillfully professional as his draw. A body rather than a head shot, the bullet drilling into the deputy's chest to find his heart. The horse had come to an unmoving halt just before the revolver exploded, and did not even twitch its ears when the shotgun roared, the finger of the dying Doonon squeezing both triggers to pepper the street surface with divot-raising shots.

As the twin barrels angled down, Doonon staggered backward: a corpse before his legs collapsed under him and he crumpled into a large heap, one hand still fisted around the shotgun.

His killer followed him down with the revolver, not sliding it back into the holster before he was certain his victim was dead. As he put the gun away, he snapped his head around to look toward a burst of vocal sound—at the batwing doors of the Lucky Lady as a tight-lipped John Boxer plunged through them, ahead of a group of shouting men.

"Hot damn, he shot Rich!" somebody yelled to end a short silence which had gripped the crowd the moment the men were on the street.

The sheriff already had his Colt out of the holster. As he heard other men draw, he snapped: "I'll handle this!" and waved his free hand to hold back the group as he strode out in front of it.

The newscomer clucked his horse into a slow advance, then brought the animal to another statue-like standstill, ten feet from where Boxer stopped. Spilled light from the doorway and windows of the saloon reached to the horse and rider.

The animal was a solid black stallion, long-legged and muscular: a horse in the prime of life and peak of condition. Maybe even a thoroughbred under the trail dust and dried sweat of a long ride.

The man astride him was past his prime. He was pushing sixty but had taken care of himself. Six feet tall and built on lean lines, there was something about the way he sat his saddle that suggested great physical strength. His face between the dangling corks emanated a brand of quiet dignity, despite the gray bristles of several days, which sprouted on his jaw and lower cheeks. Cleaned up and freshly shaved he would probably be handsome.

"You know who you just killed, mister?" Boxer growled.

The lawman was obviously aware that he had a larger audience than the group out front of the Lucky Lady and he spoke louder than necessary.

So that his words reached most of the way down Main Street to the people who had been drawn to doors and windows by the revolver shot and shotgun blast.

"Name of Richard Doonon," the rider answered, the Kentucky or perhaps Tennessee of long ago sounding in his slow-speaking voice. "My name's Dexler Grace. Doonon and me were old enemies. He may have mentioned me."

"Doonon wasn't a great one for words, mister!" Boxer snarled, angered by Grace's casual manner. "What he was was a deputy sheriff of Sun City. And no one guns down a lawman in this town and shrugs it off like all he'd done was swat a fly."

"Self-defense, Sheriff," Grace replied and nodded along the street. "Got me an eyewitness to that."

Boxer continued to keep his Colt trained on Grace as he looked back over his shoulder and saw more than fifty people peering at him.

"Guy with the rifle in front of the lit doorway on the corner," Grace expanded. "Saw it all."

The Virginian saw Boxer's face begin to form the lines of a cruel grin, then heard the sardonic laugh as the law-man turned to face Grace again. Dexler Grace was abruptly tense astride his horse.

"Mister, did you pick the wrong man for an eye-witness. That there is Adam Steele. Stranger in town like yourself. And like you, he ain't got no reason to like Rich Doonon."

"Sheriff!" the Virginian called and moved out onto the center of the intersection.

"What d'you want, Steele?"

Boxer kept his eyes and gun trained on Grace. Several of the men from the Luck Lady turned their glowering attention down Main Street.

"It happened like he said. Doonon was gunning for him. Tried to bushwack him. What I thought about Doonon doesn't alter the truth."

"Save it for the trial, Steele!" Boxer snarled.

"Frig a trial, Jack!" the Carter ranch hand named Pat snapped. "Stranger just rode into town and gunned down Rich. And maybe it wasn't no accident the punk dude being on the street. Let's string the both of them up!"

Liquor slurred his words. And there was a drunken recklessness in the shouts of agreement that rose from behind him. The short, broadly-built, red-headed Pat was the first to go for his gun. But the other three who carried revolvers were quick to copy him, pushing forward to the front of the group.

"There'll be none of that while I'm the law around here and . . ."

High anger put an adge on Boxer's voice as he swung away from Grace to glare at the group of excited drunks. But, out of the corner of his eye, he saw something which caused him to halt the move and curtail his words.

"Time to see what kind of respect the law has in this town," Dexler Grace said, and aimed his fast-drawn gun at the head of the sheriff, confident of a hit over such a short range. "Everyone

52

drops his gun or I get hung for killing two peace officers. And maybe a couple of fellers who can't take their liquor."

Steele heard footfalls behind him, but did not turn around.

"Dear God, is the killing never going to stop in this town?" Harry Andrews murmured through clenched teeth as he came to a halt beside the Virginian.

Some of the men in front of the Lucky Lady muttered their disgust and anger. Boxer dropped his Frontier Colt to the street.

"Count of three for you men," Grace warned evenly. "Still the sheriff's life on the line. If I'm alive to be strung up, guess I'll deserve it for killing an unarmed man. One . . . two . . . "

"All right!" Pat snarled, and hurled his gun viciously out across the street. The other three Carter hands, who had been watching the burly redhead nervously, discarded their revolvers in the same way.

"That feller's doing his best for you," Steele replied to the newspaperman's rhetorical question as Grace once more displayed his command of the well-schooled black stallion.

By the lightest touch of his heels against the flanks and soft spoken order, Grace caused the animal to move smoothly into reverse.

"You won't get away with this, mister!" Boxer threatened. "You'll stand trial for murderin' Rich Doonon."

"Best you make yourself scarce, Mr. Steele," Andrews advised. "If the stranger does escape, they could start looking for a scapegoat. And Pat Gundry has already planted the seed."

"A newspaperman shouldn't mix his metaphors, feller," the Virginian answered.

Just as Dexler Grace lunged himself and his mount into furious movement he exploded a shot into the ground some ten feet in front of Boxer. The report caused the men out front of the saloon to flinch and be gripped by stunning shock for a moment. Which was time for Grace to jerk his mount into a rearing wheel and then plunge him into a gallop: off the end of the street and out on to the open trail.

Boxer was closest to his gun and was the first to stoop, pick up the revolver and explode a wild shot toward the leaning forward form of the rider. The four Carter hands bumped into each other with curses ripping from their lips as they lunged across the street, snatching up the first guns which came to hand.

The sheriff took time to aim and his second shot was one of a volley that cracked through the night air in a futile attempt to stop Grace's escape. For horse and rider were far enough up the sloping trail to be out of effective revolver range.

"Get your horses!" Boxer yelled, whirling to rake his glowering eyes over the angry faces of the men with guns. "We're goin' after the sonofabitch!"

"What about Steele?" Pat Gundry snarled, and drew all attention to the center of the intersection.

Where Harry Andrews stood in lonely isolation, staring down at the spot where the Virginian had been just a few moments before.

"What the hell happened to him, Harry?" Boxer yelled, striding down the street toward the puzzled newspaperman.

He was dumbfounded by the sudden absence of Steele and could do no more than shake his head in response to the lawman's question.

In the lobby of the hotel, to which he had silently retreated while all attention was focused upon Grace's escape, the Virginian grinned at the bespectacled Myron Goldstein. The old man had backed hurriedly away from the door to allow Steele inside.

"Did you see me come through here, feller?" he asked.

"Never saw nothin'," the elderly Jew answered, stepping back to his vantage point with one of the doors cracked open. "Except for one smart man make a fool outta Jack Boxer. If another one is doin' the same thing, I sure didn't see him."

"Grateful to you," Steele said, and was careful to stay out of line with the window and glass panels of the doors as he made for the foot of the stairway and started up.

"You're welcome."

"Gundry, Hellen, Salter, Gibbs!" Boxer yelled. "You're comin' with me to get Grace. Rest of you men arm yourselves and search this town for Steele. Consider yourselves deputized. Alive'll be best, but if you have to kill him, the law'll be on your side!"

"Sheriff just proved what I've always

believed," Steele called from halfway up the stairs.

"What's that?" Goldstein answered, puzzled.

"There's Rich law and a different kind for the rest of us."

CHAPTER FIVE

Steele looked down from the window of his room upon the activity on Main Street, conscious that many other pairs of eyes were also watching from the darkness behind other windows. Boxer and his deputies were the only people in sight, the sheriff and the four Carter hands astride horses and a half dozen other men on foot. A final order was given to those assigned to search for the Virginian and then the riders heeled their mounts into a gallop that quickly took them out of his field of vision.

For a few moments after that, the toothless bartender from the Lucky Lady and five of his customers continued to stand in a group on the center of Main Street where it began its northern stretch, trying to summon back the confidence which had drained out of them as they watched Boxer gallop away. Then the sounds of a moving wagon reached the men and they took this as a signal to move, starting along Main as a group to begin the search at the northern edge of Sun City.

The wagon was that of Charlie Bennett, with the familiar form of the stoop-shouldered, pot-bellied undertaker up on the seat. Moonlight bathed the man's face and Steele was certain the features were arranged in a smile. But there was no way to tell whether the man was pleased Doonon was dead or simply feeling good at the sudden up-turn in business.

He had left the room door ajar and Helen Stewart spoke through the gap, "Adam, are you there?"

He started to whirl fast, bringing the Colt Hartford down from his left shoulder to slap the barrel into the cupped palm of his right hand. His left thumb was on the hammer but he recognized the woman's voice and did not cock the rifle.

"I'm still good for the rent," he replied.

"May I come inside?"

"You're the one with a reputation to lose," he warned. "Seems I've already blotted my copy-book."

She eased the door open just enough to pass through and then halted on the threshold. Enough moonlight entered the room at an angle to bathe her face and figure in pale blue making her look more beautiful than Steele had ever seen before. And he experienced a pang of guilt at the stirring of sexual want which churned in his lower belly. It was a momentary thing, but in its passing he acknowledged to himself that desire for this woman was the reason he was still in this town.

"Do you want to tell the world about it?" she asked.

"You've lost me, Miss Stewart."

She shrugged. "In a place like this the world doesn't stretch much further than the horizon on a hazy day. Harry wants to run the story of Doonon's death in the *News*. If he can get the paper out, everyone who lives within twenty miles of Sun City will read about what happened. Maybe the fact that a lawman here tried to gun down a man out of hand will stir a few people out of their apathy. You're the only one who saw what happened and can tell it."

Steele pursed his lips and nodded. "I recall Andrews saying that the fire hadn't put him out of business. He can still print his newspaper?"

"When Harry came to Sun City he had a press small enough to load onto a pack horse. He started the *News* with that in the basement of his house. It was only after more than a year that he was able to open the office and buy better equipment. The first press and some newsprint stock are still in the basement. He's working on a special edition right now. Your story of how Doonon died would make it extra special."

Her tone of voice was neutral, but her gray eyes expressed a tacit plea for him to agree.

"All right," he allowed, starting across the room toward her. "Boxer has already put out a contract on me. Reckon it won't do any harm for me to add some of the fine print."

She smiled her relief as she backed out into the

hallway. "And you'll be safer in Harry's basement than here, Adam."

"Reckon so, ma'am."

"I'll lead the way?"

"Following you will be a real pleasure."

As she started along the hallway he watched the sway of her hips for a few steps, then had to force himself to avert his eyes and see the woman as just one facet of his dangerous surroundings.

Down in the lobby, Myron Goldstein was back behind the desk, but he hurried to keep watch through the front doors until Helen had led Steele out of sight through the door marked PRIVATE. They went across a room furnished as an office, then down a short hallway and through a door that gave onto a courtyard between the rear of the hotel and the livery stable.

Dwight Tuxon stood in the open gateway, his head swinging from side to side, checking that the intersection and Pacific Street were clear. He held up a hand to halt them in the shadows as the familiar creak and clop of Bennett's wagon sounded on Main Street. Then, when the flatbed had rolled out of sight, he beckoned them forward and led the way across the street and through an alley between two houses.

Steele allowed free rein to his war-taught sense of being watched, but felt secure. Then the going became less tense, across the back lots of stores and houses on the east side of south Main.

Even in the moonlight and from the rear, the Andrews house stood out from its neighbors because of its state of disrepair. Windows were cracked and some panes which had fallen out had been replaced only with pieces of board. Every area of painted timber was flaking or bubbled.

The woman took over the lead from Tuxon and pulled open a door that creaked softly. No light showed inside but she entered confidently, warning those who followed to stay close to her. They crossed a cluttered kitchen smelling of grease, boiled vegetables and kerosene. Then went out into a narrow hallway where Helen came to a halt.

"Harry!" she called, her voice a rasping whisper. And rapped her knuckles on a door.

"A moment." Then: "All right, come on down."

"Be careful, the steps are steep," she warned as she opened the door and went through.

Tuxon ushered Steele ahead of him and closed the door behind him. A match was struck and touched to a lamp wick, flooding the basement with yellow light.

It was a large room, made small by clutter: a store place for household items and the paraphernalia of the printing trade with a space hurriedly cleared at the center so that the trade could be continued.

"Ah, good, he came," Andrews greeted as he stooped over a frame of typesetting, continuing the job that had engaged him before Helen knocked on the door. "Make yourself as comfortable as you can, Mr. Steele. I'll be with you as soon as I've finished setting my editorial leader."

The unrailed steps sloped down a side wall of

the basement and there was a narrow passageway from the bottom to the area where the newspaperman was at work. There were chairs in the basement, but these were piled in an inaccessible corner. Andrews was working at a desk with a small printing press to one side. There were only wooden crates and stacks of newsprint to sit on, but these were ignored.

"Well, I'll leave you to it for now," Helen said. "I'll be down again as soon as they've been."

"Get the light, son," Andrews instructed and Tuxon turned down the wick before the woman opened the door at the top of the steps, then relit the lamp again after she had closed it behind her.

"Boxer's bully boys are sure to come here," Andrews explained without looking up from his task of transferring type from trays to the frame. "Ellie will answer the door in her nightdress. The sight of her like that in my house will keep their minds on other things, I think."

Dwight started to grin, but thought better of it.

"Reckon it will," Steele agreed. "This edition of your paper will sure be a . . ."

It was a choked cry that caused the Virginian to break off in mid-sentence—the sound coming from up in the house. He, Andrews and Dwight Tuxon all snapped their heads around to look toward the top of the steps. Steele was the only one with a gun and he swung and cocked the Colt Hartford.

"It's all right!" Helen called in the same rasping whisper as before. "It's the man who killed Doonon. Put the light out, Harry."

There was horror on Andrews' face and Dwight expressed fear. Before either of them had recovered from their shock Steel reached out and turned down the lamp wick. Its charred smell filled the basement, seeming somehow to make the darkness blacker.

"All right!" Steele called, then lowered his voice. "Andrews, strike a match as soon as the door's closed."

Enough moonlight reached in through the windows of the house to allow the three men to pick the open doorway out of the surrounding dark. Steele trained his rifle on the pale rectangle.

"I mean the lady no harm," Grace promised. "Nor none of you men down there. But I got a gun on her and if I have to use it, it won't be any mistake I made."

They showed themselves in the doorway, blotting out most of the weak moonlight: the woman in front and the man close behind her. He was a foot taller than her and Steele knew he could put a bullet into the head of Grace if he had to. But he eased the hammer back to the rest and canted the rifle to his shoulder as the door closed and Andrews lit a match. In its flare the three men below received the first impression of the couple at the top of the steps, then as the lamp spread a brighter, longer lasting light, they watched the situation change.

Dexler Grace stepped away from Helen and then to the side, turning slightly so that the watchers below could see him slide his Remington revolver back into its holster.

"Sorry I had to scare you, lady," he said. "You men, too. But it seemed to me there was no other way to do it."

"Do what, feller?" Steele asked as the elderly gunman started down the steps.

Grace had something else in common with Steele—when he smiled through the dangling corks the expression took several years off his age. "Get together with some people who want the same thing as I do, Mr. Steele."

"And what is that?" Andrews countered, his tone ice cold.

"To keep Franklin Carter from gettin' richer than he is at other people's expense, Mr. Andrews."

"By killing people?" the pale-faced newspaper-man snarled as Grace reached the foot of the steps.

A shrug. "It's Carter's game I'm hornin' in on. So I have to play by the rules he makes. Mr. Steele there looks like the kind of man who can understand that?"

An inflection in his voice added the query, which he emphasized with his clear blue eyes.

"We're both hooked, feller," the Virginian answered. "You want to block or tackle?"

CHAPTER SIX

Once again the light was doused and then relit after Helen Stewart had gone through the doorway to decoy the searchers away from the basement.

"How'd you get away from the posse and sneak back into town, sir?" Dwight asked, starting the question in the darkness and completing it as Andrews touched a match to the wick.

The newspaperman, a deep-set frown of mixed anxiety and anger on his face, stooped over his typesetting work and seemed intent upon cutting himself off from everything else that was happening in the basement. Steele and the boy watched as Grace came closer and showed a first sign of weariness as he hoistedly himself up to sit on a crate of books. Dwight was excitedly interested in the newcomer. The Virginian was simply curious.

"It wasn't hard, son. Of the whole bunch—the men trailin' me and them that are on the streets—the sheriff's the only one that's professional. And the sheriff ain't no great shakes at his job, seems to me. I set my horse to runnin' free, hid until the posse went by and then walked back."

He massaged both thighs as if they still ached from the unaccustomed exercise. Then took off his hat to reveal that his gray sideburns were comprised of almost all the hair he possessed. Unshaded from the brightness of the lamp light, his face showed a thousand deeply scored lines like knife cuts in the surface of a piece of darkly stained leather.

"Men on the streets weren't lookin' for anyone tryin' to get into town. For someone already here—you, I guess, Mr. Steele?"

The Virginian nodded.

"Made for the hotel, which I figured would have plenty of empty rooms. Got there in time to see you two fellers and the lady sneak out the back. Trailed you to this house."

Nobody said anything for a full half minute, until Andrews came erect with a sigh and a crack of a bone. "All that is unimportant, if you don't mind me saying so. What interests me is why you want to put an end to Carter's plans for Sun City."

"Personal," Grace replied.

Andrews glowered his resentment of the terse answer and shared a portion of his feelings with the Virginian. "If that is as far as you are prepared to go, then I can only assume that your interest is akin to that of Steele. That you are a professional gunfighter and paradoxically share the same aim as Carter. In short, money."

Grace was not provoked to anger. He sighed wearily before replying, "Think whatever the hell you like. But know one thing, Mr. Andrews. You and me want the same thing. I'm ready to help you and it won't cost you a cent. What it might cost you is some sleepless nights on account that you don't like my methods. But you been tryin' for a year to stop Carter. Your way. And it ain't worked."

Sounds from upstairs caused Andrews to press an index finger against his lips. The gesture was unnecessary for all four had heard the bang of a fist on wood and a shout.

"What is it?" Helen called.

The man at the door shouted again, but his words were indistinct.

"Wait a moment then."

They didn't hear her footfalls, perhaps because she was barefoot. The sounds of the door being unbolted and pulled open did reach into the basement.

"Oh, it's you, Mr. Cantwell," Helen said and to the ears of the men in the basement she was giving a good impression of somebody just roused from deep sleep. "Looking for Adam Steele, I suppose?"

"Gee, Miss Stewart. I didn't mean to . . . I just wanted to . . . Jack Boxer had told us to check every place."

"You don't have to get tongue-tied, Mr. Cantwell. And you needn't look at me as if I was a schoolmistress you'd suddenly discovered was a scarlet woman."

"I didn't . . . I'm not . . . I'm sorry, Miss Stewart."

"The fact is that Harry was deeply shocked by what happened at the *News* office, Mr. Cantwell. Shocked enough to make him sick. I gave him something to make him sleep and that is what he is doing. But I was worried about him so I decided to stay the night. Tell the town gossips what you like, but I can assure you Harry is in the bedroom and I have been dozing in a chair in the parlor."

"I wouldn't tell nobody nothin', Miss Stewart."

"Then that is fine, Mr. Cantwell. I wish you a very good night. And I'll thank you to see that there is no further chance of Harry being disturbed."

"Yes, Miss Stewart. Certainly."

The door was closed and silence returned to the house. Until Dexler Grace said, "That's one cool and smart lady, Mr. Andrews."

"Who is beginning to think your way," the newspaperman growled and used the back of a hand to wipe sweat beads off his brow. The strain of standing idly by while his fiancée stalled Cantwell seemed to sap the final heeltap of energy from a reserve that had been draining away all day. His gray eyes pleaded for understanding as he swung them between the impassive faces of Grace and Steele. "But she is convinced I should be given one more try." He waved a hand over the frame of set type on the desk. "This is one page of what could be the last edition of the *Sun City News*. If that is what it proves to be, then I will admit I have failed. And I will go along with whatever you men intend to do. You are strangers here and I am part of the community. I think I deserve to be given what I ask for?"

There was a deep felt pain in Andrews' eyes, to such an extent that he seemed upon the verge of weeping.

"Came here to tell you my story, feller," Steele replied. "And Grace looks as if he's too bushed to do much more than talk for a while."

Andrews looked at the elderly man for confirmation. Grace shook his head. "You heard me tell the local sheriff Doonon and me were old enemies. I ain't prepared to say more than that. Steele saw the shootin' and knows it was a matter of me gettin' killed or me killin' Rich Doonon. The shootin's public. Why it happened is private. About you gettin' out another paper . . . ? Hell, why not? I waited a long time to get this close to Franklin friggin' Carter. I can wait a little longer without it breakin' my heart."

Relief almost brought a smile to the lips beneath the moustache. But before the expression was half born, Andrews snatched up a sheaf of yellow paper and a pencil and became tensely attentive with expectation as he gazed at the Virginian.

"Tell me, in your own words, exactly what happened at the end of Main Street."

Steele was by nature a taciturn man but he had been given a fine education in his youth and could, when necessary, express himself well. But the sight of Andrews taking notes and the knowl-

69

edge that his words would eventually appear in print acted to block his free flow. So that, after he had given a terse report of the shooting, the newspaperman had to ask questions to get him to elaborate on the bare essentials.

But Andrews showed he was an expert on this aspect of his trade and nodded his satisfaction with the interview when it was finished. He immediately began to set type into another frame.

During the questions and answers period, Dexter Grace had begun to doze, allowing his chin to drop forward onto his chest. Then the clicks as Andrews set up the typefaces served to nudge the elderly man into a deep sleep, sitting up on one crate with a shoulder resting against another.

"Make yourself useful, Dwight," the busy-fingered Andrews suggested. "Get the paper ready, uh?"

The boy nodded eagerly, anxious to have some purpose to serve.

"He's a strange one, isn't he?" the newspaper man said without looking up.

Steele's mind was elsewhere, filled with thoughts of Helen Stewart, despite his attempts to repress them as illogical. He brought his awareness back to the present and realized Andrews was talking to him about Grace.

"Met a lot like him, feller, but none of them was ever as old as he is. Don't know if I ever saw one as fast, though."

"One thing bothers me about him."

"What?"

"Doonon was a deputy sheriff in this town.

70

That gave him the right to challenge people he thought . . ."

"Doonon tried to bushwhack that feller," Steele cut in, a little impatiently. "He wasn't reckoning to arrest him."

Andrews sighed. "Sure, I believe you. But if only he'd fill us in on why they were enemies. For the *News* to do any good at all, it has to tell the truth. And not just half of it. All of it."

"I think maybe nobody'll ever get to read what you've written, Mr. Andrews," Dwight said miserably.

"What's that, son?"

The boy had had to shift a lot of crates, cartons and furniture to reach the corner where the newsprint was stacked. He had been crouching down, just the top of his head showing, when he spoke. Now, as Andrews shot the query at him, he straightened and held up a thick wad of white, yellow-edged paper.

Not until Steele saw the many holes chewed through the newsprint did he smell the rancid odor of mouse droppings.

"Oh, sweet Jesus!" Andrews groaned, slumping down into a previously unused chair behind the desk and dropping his head into his cupped palms.

"It's all that way, son?" Steele asked.

"Yes, sir." He dropped the paper he held and lifted up another wad. "There ain't enough good stuff left to keep a privy goin' for a week."

Steele began to catch other scents in the air, lurking just behind the strongest smell of the kerosene lamp. Damp, decay and rot. And it now seemed obvious that the basement should be this way—in view of the fact that it was beneath a house that was neglected.

"Looks like it will have to be our way, feller."

Andrews raised his head and started a nod of miserable agreement. Then abruptly he was struck by an idea that flooded hope into his eyes. "No!" His excitement switched from Steele to Dwight Tuxon and back again. "The *San Varas Journal*! We can buy some newsprint off Ed Logan."

Dwight's face lit with a higher degree of excitement than that of the older man's. "Sure, Mr. Andrews! You and him have helped out each other in the past."

"Sure we have!" Andrews said, too loud. His agreement jerked Dexler Grace out of his sleep.

"What's happenin'?" he muttered, looking at the impassive Steele and the excited man and the boy with red-rimmed eyes. "You two look like we've already won."

"Different game now, feller," the Virginian told him.

Grace tried to blink the last vestiges of sleep out of his confused mind.

Steele grinned wanly. "A paper chase."

CHAPTER SEVEN

The press-ganged group of deputies had abandoned their search for Steele and the Lucky Lady Saloon was doing good business again, supplying bottled courage to men who were not looking forward to telling Sheriff John Boxer they had failed.

With the exception of the saloon and the lobby of the Sun City Hotel, the town was in complete darkness. And almost totally silent.

At first, as Steele and Grace moved away from Andrews' house and back-tracked to the hotel livery stable, they watched each other as closely as they searched for the first sign of danger. Strangers in a threatening situation, neither sure of how the other would respond if the menacing shadows became suddenly peopled with men who meant them harm.

But by the time they reached the livery they felt easier in each other's company for there had been no need for words or signs to be exchanged.

They were silently cautious by instinct and if either experienced fear, he did not allow it to show.

While Steele saddled his own gray gelding, Grace put Dwight Tuxon's gear on the boy's ageing stallion. The older man expressed mild contempt as he did this and the look remained on his craggy face as they led the horses out of town, heading north east, the sounds of the animals' progress muffled by wads of cloth tied around their hooves.

Once over the rise to the north of Sun City, the men stooped to remove the muffles.

"That stallion you were riding will take a lot of replacing, feller," Steele said as they swung up into their saddles and heeled their mounts forward.

"Hopin' I won't have to do that. He oughta be able to take care of himself until I get a chance to go out and look for him. Put a lot of work into trainin' him since I retired."

The Virginian looked at the older man, expecting him to continue. But Grace said nothing more: simply asked for a canter from his mount and got it. Steele matched the pace and the two men became concerned only with their surroundings and the possibility of running into Boxer and his deputies.

It was pleasant country: a strip of coastal plain between the San Bernardino Mountains and the Pacific Ocean. Featured with rolling hills and stands of semi-tropical timber. The moon-whitened trail from Sun City to San Varas took the line of least resistance across the terrain, sometimes looping far to the east or west to pass close by one of the many small farmsteads that were spread over the landscape.

Steele and Grace stayed to the west of the trail for most of the time, crossing it only when it made one of these wide sweeps toward the ocean. By tacit agreement, Steele kept watch to the north and east, Grace to the south and west. The old man dictated the pace because he was riding the weaker horse. The animals were never galloped and they were walked more than they were cantered.

"You know what I think, Steele?" Grace said when they had covered some three miles and were riding easy through sand dunes behind the beach, the Pacific surf beating rhythmic time over to their left.

"I'm not a mind reader, feller. But that doesn't mean I'm stupid. Boxer and his posse haven't been trailing a riderless horse all this time."

Grace grinned through the cords and corks swinging from his hat brim. "Stupid is a word that never occurred to me to use about you. I figure we don't have to tell each other what's obvious. Right?"

The Virginian nodded and showed a grin of his own. "Reckon you been thinking the same as me, feller."

"What happened to the posse? Yeah, I've been thinkin' about that. But I've got advantages you ain't. Unless you rode into town from the north. Did you?"

"From the south."

Grace nodded. "We're on Carter land now. The Pacific Ranch he calls it. Stretches more than eight miles along the coast and ten miles inland. The trail is the only public right of way across the spread." He shook his head, setting the corks to swinging more violently. "Sorry, Steele. I've done my homework but that's no reason why I should spout off to you. I figure the posse wound up at Carter's house. And raised some help."

"How far to the house?"

"Couple of miles." He extended his arms to point slightly east of north. "A real plush place built on top of a hill. Should be able to see it when we get over that next rise."

"How many men work for Carter?"

"This time of year, just the dozen regular hands." He interrupted his survey of the country to show Steele another grin. "Doing homework helps, don't it?"

"How long have you been doing it, feller?"

"About a month."

"I only rode into Sun City this morning. Didn't know I was going to do anything but rest up until this afternoon. Things have been a little hectic since then."

"Don't you care who's right or wrong, Steele?"

The Virginian felt a flame of anger flicker into life. Because of the question and of a memory it sprang into the forefront of his mind—a memory of a violent trip aboard a riverboat when he had accepted a job without questioning the morality of what he was doing.

"I've seen both sides in operation," he replied after a short pause during which he was able to suppress the urge to anger. "Just happen to like better the side that offered me a job."

Dexler Grace was setting the course as well as the pace. They had swung inland, to go around a rise rather than over it and be skylined. They reined their mounts to a halt and looked toward the house of Franklin Carter and its immediate surroundings. It was a two-storey stone built mansion squatting on a flat-topped hill. Ornamental gardens spread down the slopes. The work-aday buildings of the ranch—barns, stables, the bunkhouse—were huddled at the foot of the southern slope, surrounded on three sides by neatly fenced corrals.

The house was in darkness but there were lights gleaming among the buildings below. In the glow of the lamps it was possible to see a group of horses, still saddled, hitched to a rail beside a water trough.

"And they say crime doesn't pay!" Grace rasped venomously.

"That much hate isn't good for a man to carry around, feller," Steele said. "It can make you do something you might regret."

While he looked at the house across half a mile of lush pastureland, Grace had worked an expression of ugly malevolence on to his face. When he snapped his head around to look at Steele, it was still there: gained strength as he pulled back his thin lips to snarl a retort. But there wasn't time."

"Move again and you're dead!" somebody else snarled. "Both of you!"

The Virginian and the man filled with hatred froze, gazing into each other's face for part of a second. Then they turned their eyes to the limit of the sockets to search out the man who had spoken.

He was in a waist-high patch of brush to the right, coming erect with a Winchester rifle aimed at Grace over a range of forty feet.

"Regan ain't just talkin' to hear his own voice."

This man was to the left, out of the field of vision to the two riders. But both were aware that there was a scattering of boulders in that direction. The closest fifty feet away.

"Figured that," Grace replied.

"Like for you to get down off the horses," Regan said, breaking brush as he stepped out into the clear and came to a halt thirty feet from Grace. "Slow and easy. Grace my side and the dude on Holcombe's side. You can't see him, but Holcombe's got a rifle aimed at you, dude."

"Reckoned he might, feller."

They dismounted in the way Regan demanded, and were able to see their captors clearly. Both men in their late twenties, dressed like ranch hands and armed with holstered Colts as well as the aimed Winchester rifles. Tall, powerfully built men who were not quite able to keep the tension of nervousness off their bristled features.

"Fine," Regan said. "Now drop your guns."

"Dude ain't carryin'," Holcombe reported.

"So he don't have to drop no gun then!" Regan rasped, his tenseness finding some kind of outlet in irritation with his partner. "Both of you step forward, away from the horses."

Steele waited for Grace to discard his Remington and to make the first move. Then joined the older man six feet ahead of where the two horses dipped their heads to crop at grass.

"I got hate for an excuse," Grace said scornfully. "What's your story about not spottin' these two boys?"

"Reckon they were just too good for me, feller."

"Cut out the talkin'!" Regan snapped. "Save your breath for the walk over to the ranch. And for the talk Mr. Carter'll want to hear from you. Now turn around and move."

The Carter men had come together at the horses, their rifles never for a moment wavering off target. Just before he and Grace started to carry out the latest instruction, Steele noticed that the slightly shorter Holcombe—who was still covering him—took up the reins of both horses. Which meant he now had the rifle in a single-handed grip.

They moved along a broad gully between the high ground overlooking the beach and another rise. For several yards there was just grass under their feet, muting the footfalls of men and animals. Then they started across a broad area of hard and cracked dirt scattered with pebble and small rocks. A dry wash, that started on the eastern slop, ran along the gully and then curved to the left, showing how the water of a Californian storm found its way to the ocean in this piece of territory.

"No way you could've seen me and Holcombe," Regan said, still nervous, as small pebbles rolled and rattled under boots and hooves. "We was watchin' you for over a mile. Been the same whichever way you tried to make the house. Mr. Carter's got every way from the south guarded. Our luck you come this way."

"Luck?" Steele posed.

"Me and Holcombe get to earn a hundred bucks each, dude." The prospect of money eased his mind and lightened his tone.

"Dead or alive," Holcombe added and he sounded as anxious as ever.

"Yeah, dead or alive," Regan agreed.

Steele did not disbelieve the men. But knew that he and Grace would be considered a greater prize alive. Which gave him added confidence when he began the pretense of an accidental plunge to the stone littered ground.

"Regan!"

"What the frig?"

The shouts of the two men exploded ice cold fear from the pit of his stomch to reach every nerve ending. And he knotted his muscles in expectation of shots and the impact of bullets thudding into his body. He kicked at stones as he forced his right leg out from under himself, sending them skittering noisily across the ground.

Grace looked as surprised as the two Carter

80

hands sounded—and made a grab at Steele. But the Virginian evaded the reaching hands and hit the ground on his right side, his right leg bent so that the split seam in his pants gaped wide. Just before he crashed painfully into a heap, forcing a groan of agony through his gritted teeth, he delved his hand into the opening and withdrew it—the wooden handle of a knife in his fist.

No shots exploded and the only pain he felt was from the self-inflicted fall: this not so intense as his groan had indicated.

"Hold it, Holcombe!" Regan snarled. "What's the damn idea, dude?"

The Carter hands had come to an abrupt halt. So had Grace. The fifteen feet distance between captors and captives remained unchanged.

"Seems like it's not my night," the Virginian said, answering Regan's question but looking at the now impassive Grace and winking the eye that was on the blind side of the riflemen as he feigned difficulty in forcing himself up into a sitting posture. He placed the knife on the ground beside his leg, out of sight of Regan and Holcombe. "I think I've twisted my ankle."

Grace was intrigued, but did not allow it to show for more than a moment as he stooped to hook a hand under Steel's armpit. His other hand went lower, to pick up the knife and push it dangerously into his pants pocket.

"Try and get up on it, buddy," the older man said.

"You better be able to!" Regan threatened.

"And to walk on it. All the way to the ranch. You ain't got no chance of gettin' back on your horse."

"Accidents happen, feller," Steele said, then lowered his voice to the merest whisper as he allowed Grace to take his weight and haul him to his feet. "Wait for my signal."

His right leg, hip and shoulder ached from hitting the stone-scattered ground. But he pretended the sole source of pain was his right ankle as he attempted to put his foot down and acted another groan.

"Don't worry about it," Grace tossed over his shoulder as he took a firmer grip on Steele. "We'll make it. Slow, but we'll make it."

"You better!" Regan warned, the threat lacking power.

They started forward, Dexler Grace proving he was as strong as he looked, for, on every other step, Steele threw all his weight onto the older man, who accepted it without any sign of strain.

The Virginian had forced his fall thirty yards back from where the gully ended, at the side of the broad pastureland that stretched all the way to the ranch buildings. Steele made heavy going over half this distance and Regan and Holcombe found it difficult to maintain the fifteen feet gap, they and the horses finding the pace unnaturally slow.

"Drop me, but wait," Steele whispered.

Grace did just that. He allowed his supporting arm to sag and the Virginian sank back to the ground.

"Jesus Christ!" Regan growled, exasperated.

Steele and Grace were both half turned to look back at the riflemen, who had closed to within eight feet of them. Both Winchesters were aimed steadily on the same targets as before.

"If you get to my age, son, see if you do better," Grace muttered wearily. He pushed both hands into his pockets.

Steele rubbed the side of his neck.

The bright moonlight shafting into the gully showed exhaustion on the face of Grace and pain in the set of Steele's features. Regan and Holcombe were anxious.

"Hell, you stay here and guard them," Holcombe suggested. "I'll ride to the ranch and bring back help."

"Frig that!" his partner snapped. "They're ours. We got them. We'll bring them in. Leave the horses and back off. Grace, you haul your dude buddy over here and put him on his horse."

"We weren't gonna do that, Regan." Holcombe complained.

"I know we weren't! But it's changed now."

"What about the rifle in the boot, Regan?"

The taller of the Carter hands glowered at his partner. "Take the friggin' rifle outta the friggin' boot, dummy!"

The Virginian had planned his second fall so that he was in a perfect posture to rise fast and power toward the riflemen. And ever since he was down he had been poised to launch a life-or-death attack. He had not chanced a glance at the man standing over him: could only hope that

Grace's apparent exhaustion was completely fake and that his reactions would be as fast now as when he had spotted and host Rich Doonon.

"Time!" he rasped.

Holcombe was reaching for and then grasping the stock of the Colt Hartford jutting up from the boot on the saddle of the gray gelding. Regan was still glowering his anger at the shorter man's inability to think for himself.

Steele powered up into a half crouch and lunged across the ground—his right hand whipping away from the side of his neck, fisted around one corner of his silk kerchief.

Grace kept both feet firmly on the ground: merely swung his body around from the waist as he drew both hands from his pockets.

The Virginian experienced a fleeting rise of anger that he had not known the older man could throw a knife. Then his emotion was swamped by icy fear of death as the heads of Regan and Holcombe snapped around. They were afraid, too. Shocked by the sudden move and terrified of what result it might have.

They saw Grace's arm reach the limit of a powerful throwing action and moonlight glint on the object he had hurled toward them. And they saw the Virginian closing on them with incredible speed—whirling something above his head.

The abruptness of their own moves had caused the rifles in their hands to waver. And instinctively they stepped back, which wasted another vital instant of time.

It was the final part of a second left to Holcombe. For the blade of the knife thudded deep into his chest before his back step was completed. He uttered a grunt of surprise at the impact and then opened his mouth wide to scream as his punctured heart exploded agony to every nerve ending in his body. But only the death rattle sounded in his throat as he fell backward.

Steele should have died at precisely the same moment, of a rifle bullet blasted into his chest over a range of two feet. But the nervousness which he had always known was gripping Regan gave the Virginian an advantage he had not even hoped for.

Regan gasped and squeezed the Winchester trigger. Then groaned when nothing happened. The hammer was not cocked.

"Lucky bastard," Grace growled.

Regan got his thumb on to the hammer. But it was too late then.

Steele lashed his left arm out to the side, knocking the rifle barrel out of the way and off target. Then he skidded to a halt and gave his right arm one more turn, bending it at the elbow.

Regan stumbled into a backward fall, terror contorting the moonlighted lines of his face. His fear expanded, widening his eyes and baring his teeth as he felt something curl around the back of his neck.

Steele's left hand came up as if to strike Regan, but the Carter man felt only the slipstream as the half formed fist missed his jaw by a fraction of an inch. The fist became fully clenched, gripping another corner of the silk kerchief. Then the Virginian interlocked his elbows and pulled his crossed-over arms as wide as he could.

Regan began to die: his throat constricted by no ordinary Western kerchief. Instead, an Oriental weapon of assassination—a scarf with two diagonally opposite corners weighted. Something Adam Steele had learned to use in those opening days of the violent peace as he tracked down the men who lynched his father.

Only the Virginian's strength kept Regan on his feet as the dying man lost the use of his muscles—dropping the rifle and lifting his hands to claw at the scarf as his legs buckled.

Steele gazed impassively into Regan's face as the eyes widened still further and bulged and the lips formed an enormous circle, the mouth trying to suck in life-giving air. The final dregs of energy drained out of the man's arms and he dropped them to his sides.

The dirt and sweat-stained length of silk cut deep into Regan's neck, becoming almost buried under the flesh that swelled above and below it.

The Virginian knew he had won. That he could have relaxed his two-handed grip on the scarf and that Regan would sink to the ground, helpless and on the brink of unconsciousness. But that was not good enough. Regan had to die to leave Steele feeling satisfied: exonerated in his own mind from the shame of being captured so easily by a pair of amateurs.

Regan's mouth closed and his bulging eyes became glazed over with the film of death.

Steele heard pebbles rattling behind him, then the tap of Dexler Grace's hand on his shoulder.

"You can let him be now," the older man growled. "It's you got a lot of hate this time. And him that could lose his head on account of it."

The Virginian unclenched his gloved left hand and the corpse crumpled into a heap at his feet. The thuggee's scarf hung loosely in the air above the dead man. Grace stooped, put a foot on the belly of Holcombe and withdrew the knife from the chest. Blood spurted from the hole. Not much of it. He wiped the blood from the blade on his own pants leg before handing the knife back to Steele.

He grinned. "You ain't by any chance got a Gatling gun tucked inside your vest pocket?"

The Virginian hung the scarf back around his neck and replaced the knife in his boot sheath before responding to the grin with one of his own.

"Do you know any other tricks apart from throwing a knife, feller?"

The older man vented a short laugh. "Thought I knew them all. But the way you killed that guy . . . well, that sure was something'."

Steele looked wryly down at the crumpled corpse of Regan. "Kind of choked him up, too."

CHAPTER EIGHT

Dexler Grace looked across the pasture at the house on the hill and the buildings below.

"Yeah, that's him," he said at length.

"Who?"

"My horse. One of them tied up by the trough. Figure the posse caught up with him and the sheriff decided to ride right on out and tell Carter about me."

"You ready to tell me about you, feller?" Steele asked as Grace turned around and took the reins of his borrowed horse from the gloved hand.

"Guess there's no reason not to," the older man replied. "Never was a reason. Let's go back, get my gun and ride around the blind side of the hill."

He stooped to claim Regan's Winchester and slid it into the empty boot on his saddle. Then they led the horses along the gully to where they had been captured. And he picked up the Remington and replaced it in his holster as if the revolver was something very precious to him.

Steele could understand this, even though the

gun was older and more battle-scarred than his Colt Hartford. He guessed the elderly revolver had saved Grace's life on more than one occasion, and maybe had killed some men the owner needed to see dead.

They had to ride along the sandy beach to stay out of sight of the Carter house, and they rode easy, confident that the only two men watching for their passing in this area were dead.

"See this?" Grace asked suddenly.

Steele turned toward him as the older man lifted a lapel of his jacket to display the dented and rusted five-pointed tin star that was pinned there.

"You're a lawman?"

"Was. Like I told you, I've retired."

"Whereabouts?"

"Up in the north of this state. Little town called Carterville on the Trinity River. Anyway, was called that while I was lawman there. On account of it was owned lock, stock and barrel by Franklin Carter."

"Not a good town to live in?"

"Not unless you was a Carter man. And I was. It was a wide open town with everyone that lived in it makin' a pile of money from the folks that had to do business in town. Small time farmers and ranchers at the start. But then there was a gold strike. Nothin' real spectacular but there was paydirt there. And like most place else men find gold, they were real anxious to turn it into spendin' money and spend it. And Franklin Carter supplied whatever it was the men wanted to buy.

Women, liquor, games of chance. At real high prices. And when a man was broke, Carter gave credit. At real high interest rates."

Grace leaned to the side and spat into the sand. "He got real rich real quick. And I helped him." The man seemed to grow older with each word he spoke, his tone getting more bitter. "Takin' over the gold claims for him when the miners couldn't meet payments on the loans. And some of them guys were real big and real mean. Had to kill some of them when they wouldn't yell uncle. But I got paid well and I had me a bunch of deputies to help out when the goin' got real rough. And a tame judge that was always on the side of the law."

He became silent for a long time, peering out across the moon-silvered ocean and allowing his mind to relive bad memories.

Steele thought there was a danger of him withdrawing into secrecy again. "I reckon you didn't just see the error of your ways," he nudged.

"Sure didn't," Grace agreed with a sigh. "Got me a woman. Young and pretty and a whore. But she got to me, Steele. Real hard. That ever happen to you?"

"Never did."

"Well, there ain't no use explainin' somethin' like that to a man who ain't never experienced it. I figured she felt the same about me as I did about her. But she was stringin' me along. To get close to Carter and make a play for him. Which is what she did. And he took her away from me, Steele. By that time he owned every claim around his town and was running a company to bring out what was left of the paydirt. But the bastard didn't own me. Just my woman. I told her she'd be like all the others he bedded, Steele. That she'd last as long as it took him to find another one he liked better. But she wouldn't buy that. So I shot her."

"Just like that?"

Grace sighed again. "I told you there's no way you can understand. Pearl was my whole life and I lost her to Carter. I knew she'd be happy for a time, but then he'd kick her out. I didn't want her to suffer that, so I shot her. Made it easy for her. In the back of the head so she didn't expect it." He clicked a finger against his thumb. "She died like that. Could have killed myself or Carter. Maybe the both of us. But that would have left her alive to maybe feel blame."

He spat again to the side and pulled himself more erect in the saddle. "Anyway, Carter was a man who didn't like losin' anythin' that was his. And he gave me an hour to leave town or stand trial for murder. There were too many guns against me to do anythin' except leave. And they trailed me with a lynch rope. The men who had been my deputies. Six of them. Killed every one of them except Rich Doonon who was only a kid then. This was seven years ago. Couldn't kill him on account of he ran away too damn fast."

They had been riding up the slope of a rocky promontory which curved out into the ocean, its outward end surrounded by the angry white water of breakers. At the top, Grace said:

"We're off the Pacific range now. Outside of the Sun City sheriff's jurisdiction."

"Should that make me feel secure, feller?" Steele asked.

"Carter's got too much to lose."

Far ahead and to the east, a light gleamed between the fold of two hills. Grace altered course to head for the distant beacon.

"I been driftin' all over since then, Steele. Tryin' to get Pearl outta my mind. But no matter what I did or where I went the memory of her was still there gnawin' away at my mind. I drank too much, smoked too much and whored too much. Was real sick a lot of the time. Until I figured there was only one thing that might work for me. So I came back to California. Went to Carterville first, but that ain't there no more. Just a few fallen down buildin's to show where it used to be.

"So I did some more driftin', until I picked up the word about Carter livin' down here in the south of the state. Heard he'd put his money into the Pacific spread, but I knew he wouldn't be happy to just put his feet up. His greed would never let him do that. Then I did some checkin' and found out about his plans for Sun City. And for a while I figured that maybe I was wrong. That all he was after was some fame to go along with his fortune. Until I happened to see a copy of Harry Andrews' newspaper and read about what some of the local folks thought of Carter's plans. So I did some more checkin' and then rode on down here."

Once more he spat to the side, the globule of saliva hitting the lush grass instead of sand now. And there was in the gesture a signal of finality: a tacit indication that he had said as much as he intended to say.

"You still plan to kill him, feller?" Steele probed.

"My business."

"Reckon you don't. Or you wouldn't be running errands for Harry Andrews."

"Leave it, Steele," Grace growled. "Ain't you ever been undecided in your life?"

"Almost every day," the Virginian drawled softly and the two men began another long silence, which lasted until they joined the trail just outside the single street town of San Varas.

Like Sun City, this smaller community had been established to serve the needs of the farmers, growers and stock raisers who lived and worked on small plots of land scattered over the surrounding country between the mountains and the ocean. But it was not so prosperous as the town to the south and there was a weary, forlorn look about the frame buildings which faced each other across the optimistically wide street.

The light which had acted as a beacon to the two riders had probably been left burning in error. It shone out through the single window of the town's saloon, midway down the eastern side of the unnamed street.

"Newspaper office is down at the far end on the left," Dexler Grace said. "Came through San

Varas on the ride south. Don't see no point in wakin' anybody, do you?"

"Ride around?"

"Gotta be the best way."

They angled their horses off the trail and rode wide around the back lots of the buildings on the western side of the street. Both watched and listened intently for a sign that the clop of hooves had roused a light sleeper. But they reached the rear of the *Journal* office without attracting attention.

"You ain't been paid and maybe never will be," Grace murmured as they dismounted and hitched their horses to a flatbed wagon. "I know what I figure to get outta this set-up. So you watch and I'll do the stealin'."

His soft-spoken words were mere scratches on the silence which had pervaded the depressed and depressing town since the gelding and the stallion were tethered. But they were not loud enough to mask a sharp intake of breath and the sound of a booted foot being put to the ground.

Grace drew and whirled and Steele powered into a half-turn, slapping the barrel of the Colt Hartford down into his cupped hand. The hammers of the Remington and the rifle were cocked in perfect unison and both men took first pressure against their triggers. Both muzzles were trained upon a short, fat, bearded man who came into view out of the shadows at a corner of the newspaper building. He held his arms out in front of him, fingers splayed to show that he did not carry a weapon.

"You men want to steal from me, you'll have to kill me to do it," the squat, fifty-year-old man said evenly. "Name's Ed Logan. I own the local paper. Guess you people are Grace and Steele."

"You got the word," Grace said.

"Couple of hours ago. Man called Steve Salter who works for Carter. Deputy to Jack Boxer tonight."

"Sun City law doesn't stretch this far," Grace pointed out as Steele shouldered his rifle, easing the hammer back to the rest.

Logan nodded as he came to a halt in the same patch of moonlight that shone on his unwelcome visitors. "Salter said it wasn't a legal matter. But it's general knowledge the *Journal* needs new plant. And that the paper will go broke before I can earn enough to buy it."

"And you'd rather die first?" Grace asked, his aim still steady on the chest of the fat newspaperman over a range of six feet.

"The *Journal* is my life. If I lose that, I've got nothing."

"Crazy," Grace muttered.

"I reckon he doesn't have a woman," Steele said.

The older man grimaced.

The Virginian spoke again before Grace could voice the feelings he was showing. "Harry Andrews has got ink in his blood as well, feller," he said to Logan.

"I know that, mister." The fat man had the kind of face that probably always looked sad. Now the lines of this familiar expression deepened. "I like

Harry and I'd be pleased to help him out if I could. They burned him out and Salter told me to expect him to come by and try to print on my press. But I'm a selfish man. Like most in this kind of crisis. It's a matter of the *Journal* or the *News* and there aren't many men who'd have to think very much about what to do."

"Andrews is hopin' to finish Carter if he can get out another edition, Logan," Grace pressed.

The newspaperman scowled. "Not in a million years."

Grace nodded. "The way I feel, too. But the man wants to try."

"Not with my press."

"Just need some newsprint," Steele corrected.

"Same thing. I need Carter money. Not Carter trouble."

Grace glanced at Steele, setting the dangling corks into another disconcerting swing motion across his face. "Looks like we have to kill him. One more won't make any difference, I guess."

Logan had dropped his arm to his sides. The only sign of fear he showed was an opening and closing of his pudgy fists.

"Wake the whole town if we shoot him," Steele replied.

"You know the quiet ways."

The Virginian nodded and moved in a half circle to get behind Logan—who began to display another sign of the true feelings which lurked behind his almost serene veneer. His lower lip started to tremble.

"You're worse than Carter and his crowd," he

said his voice as calm as ever. "Harry wouldn't agree with you doing his dirty work this way."

"Stay friends with Andrews," Steele drawled as he closed in on the broad back of Logan. "Tell him this was your idea. To make it look good in the event Carter comes out on top."

The fat man was not wearing a hat, so there was nothing but thinning gray hair to soften the blow as the barrel of the Colt Hartford cracked into the left side of his skull. A small spurt of blood jumped from the tiny split in the skin as Logan crumpled to the ground. But the bruise which would rise later would provide more painful and longer-lasting evidence that the newspaperman had attempted to defend his premises.

"Why didn't I think of that?" Grace asked as he slid the Remington back into his holster.

"I reckon because you only see black and white, feller," the Virginian answered. "Sometimes in between there is some gray."

"You know something, Steele," the older man said as he went onto his haunches beside the raggedly breathing Logan and delved into the fat man's pockets.

"What?"

"I figure that at heart you're really a do-gooder."

He straightened up with a bunch of keys in his hand and a grin on his face.

"Depends which side I'm on, feller. Right now all I want to do is spread the good *News*."

CHAPTER NINE

One of the keys on the bunch fitted the lock on the big rear door of the *Journal* office and Dexler Grace went inside while Steele kept watch on Logan and listened for any sound to break the silence clamped over San Varas.

Four times the older man went into and out of the building, on each trip bringing from inside a large stack of newsprint, cut in a size to print two sheets of a broad-sheet newspaper.

These were loaded two apiece on the horses, hung over their necks. Then, with the *Journal's* owner still unconscious but breathing easier, Steele and Grace left town by the same route they had entered. And back-tracked on the way they had approached from Sun City.

Everything was precisely as it had been before, until they came within sight of the Carter mansion and the buildings below it. Now, no horses were hitched to the water trough and the whole place was in darkness. Then, when they reached the gully where two men had died, it was as if nothing had ever happened there.

Neither rider uttered a word as he maintained his constant watch over the moonlit and shadowed Carter spread: each reasonably sure of why the other held his silence.

The situation had changed and it was in the hands of the enemy to make the next move. But there were no indications from which either Steele or Grace could try to predict what that move would be. To make guesses would be futile. So all they could do was complete the job Andrews had set them and watch for the first sign of the enemy's move.

And with each yard they covered to close in on Sun City, the strain of the constant vigilance mounted. They blinked too often, their throats became dry and their muscles ached. Steele rode with a gloved hand only an inch from where the stock of the Colt Hartford jutted from the saddle boot while Grace actually gripped the butt of his holstered Remington. The features of both men were sheened with sweat despite the pleasantly cool after-midnight air that flowed in off the ocean.

Each was uncomfortably aware that the other knew of his tension, but neither spoke of this until the rise to the north of town came into sight.

Then Dexler Grace growled, "Why the frig didn't we hit the rest of the Carter bunch after killin' them two in the gully, Steele?"

"As easy as that, feller?" the Virginian answered with a question.

"That's your way as well as mine. Do unto others before they do it to you. All this damn pussyfootin' around gets on a man's nerves."

"That why you wore that crazy hat of yours, feller? Because you knew any man who worked for Carter in the old days would recognize you right off and start the ball rolling."

"I like the hat, Steele. But yeah, I figured it would help to stir up the crap pretty soon. Only thing is, I didn't follow through after Doonon. I could've handled the Sun City posse the same way I did the one that came outta Carterville after me. Like you said, easy as that. Same as it would have been out at the ranch awhile back. Man who hits first always has the edge. Which is why I ain't happy ridin' along like this waitin' for somebody to take first crack at me."

The Virginian agreed with the principle of what Grace was saying because his experience of violence in war and peace had always borne out the maxim of attack being the best form of defense. And, allied to this, was the fact that he was by nature a man of action when a situation called for action. But he could not go along with the older man's need for wholesale, wanton slaughter. Which was as much a reason for Steele's tenseness as the threat of a killing shot exploding out of the night.

"You want to dump the paper right here and ride into Sun City shooting, Grace?" he asked softly.

"Damn right!" came the rasping reply. Then he paused, taking the time to bring himself under control and to moderate his tone. "And so would you, I figure. But we can't do that, can we? On account of there ain't no way we could tell the black from the white and the gray."

He expressed a sardonic grin through the dangling corks.

"Times have changed, feller. For me this isn't the war when all I had to do was kill Yankees. And for you it's not Carterville when anyone who wasn't a Carter man . . ."

"Yeah, yeah, I know that," Grace cut in bitterly. "But it ain't so easy for me to keep that in mind. Only trouble I've had to handle for a lot of years has been inside my own head. And in all that long the only times I drew and fired my gun was to keep in practice. But you, you're a man who's had plenty of opportunity to change his style, I figure."

"Everyone has to start somewhere," Steele replied, reflecting briefly on the wanton slaughter he had employed as he tracked down the men who lynched his father.

They reached the foot of the incline which led to the rise overlooking Sun City and started up, heading diagonally across the slope toward a patch of brush and timber at the side of the trail just below the crest. It was the final area of cover before the town itself and, in unison, with no word spoken or sign given, both men took out their guns and rode with eyes and muzzles trained unwaveringly on the menacing area of deep shadows beneath the trees.

"Don't shoot! It's me!"

As the first word started to be rasped, the barrels of the rifle and the revolver were raked around to aim at a close growing group of leaning yuccas on the left. But before the riders could take first pressure against the triggers, they recognized the hoarse, recently broken voice of Dwight Tuxon.

Steele and Grace had both halted their mounts. Now they heeled them into slow movement.

"You alone, son?" the older man asked.

"No. I'm here too," Helen Stewart announced from behind the same cluster of trees.

The boy showed himself first, stepping nervously to the side and forward. The woman was a moment behind him. They were dressed in dark clothing so that only the paleness of their faces and hands could be seen against the shadows.

"Our plans have changed," Helen said tensely as Steele booted his rifle and Grace holstered his handgun.

"Don't do anything rash," the Virginian advised lightly as he swung down from his saddle. "It's the moonlight and the trees. The kid's too young for you. Stick with Andrews."

"This is no joking matter!" she countered angrily, making to advance out of the trees.

But Steele and Grace, who had also dismounted, forced her deeper into the shadows as they led their horses forward.

"Realize that, ma'am," the Virginian admitted, having once more to struggle to suppress a stir of sexual desire for the beautiful blonde woman.

"But if Grace and I didn't try to laugh we might cry."

"Cut it out, Steele," the older man snapped. He finished hitching the reins of the stallion to a branch and gazed expectantly at Helen. "What's happened?"

"After you left, Harry started to worry. Lots of people in town know he began the *News* from his house. He thought you might run into trouble crossing Carter land—even be caught and talk. So we managed to move the press and frames down to a cave in back of the beach. We sent Dwight up here to tell you about it if you got through."

"We got through," Steele muttered. "What else?"

"Franklin Carter and all his men are in town and Carter's trying to beat us with our own weapons after you killed those two hands of his."

She was trying to remain calm, but her voice had begun to rise and she was trembling.

"It was that or be caught," Grace growled.

"I didn't think you did it for the hell of it," she snapped. "But it gives Carter the whiphand now. I stayed in town after getting back from the cave. To see if anything happened. And it certainly did. Boxer came back along with Carter and every man off the Pacific Ranch. Including the two dead men tied to their horses. They woke everybody up and held a meeting in the middle of town. I was hiding in the hotel so I saw and heard everything. Or everything I needed to hear before

I sneaked out of town to tell Harry and then came up here."

She had started to speak too fast, running some of her words together in her haste to get them out. Finally she had to pause for breath.

"Carter's the knight in shinin' armor and we're the dragons, uh?" Grace asked.

Helen grimaced. "What do you think? There was a town deputy dead in Bennett's funeral parlor who everyone knew about. And the bodies of the two ranch hands slumped across their saddles for all to see. One stabbed and one strangled. How can words printed in a newspaper have a greater influence than that?"

"What I've been sayin' all along," Grace answered with a shrug.

"Matter of spoken lies and printed truth, seems to me" Steele countered. "Then the people who listen and read have to decide for themselves."

The woman looked at him scornfully through the darkness. "That's Harry's view. Put almost word for word."

"Never have claimed to have the edge on originality," the Virginian responded evenly.

"Carter win over the local folks?" Grace wanted to know, his tone of voice suggesting he was indifferent to the answer.

"I didn't stay in town long enough to find out. But my guess is he did. Those two men you killed tonight aren't gunfighters like you. They were just ordinary working people like most of those in town. Carter's line of attack was that if Holcombe and Regan can be murdered by hired kill-ers, so can anyone else."

"Any mention made of the feller Doonon shot in the Lucky Lady?" Steele asked. "Or the one who fired the newspaper office?"

"Yes! Doonon shot Carl Parton in self-defense for resisting a peace officer. And what Bart Dixon did was because of a personal matter. Both explanations smell worse than skunk. But we're the guilty ones until we can prove our inno-cence."

"What's the situation in town now?" the Vir-ginian asked.

"Quiet, sir," Dwight reported, eager to have something useful to contribute to the talk. "I've been spendin' my time going back and forth through this wood while Miss Helen watched for you and Mr. Grace. After the meetin' broke up folks stood around talkin' for awhile. Then went on home, it looked from up here. Except for some that went with the sheriff and Carter and his men into the hotel."

"Some?" Grace asked.

"Eight, I'd guess," Helen supplied. "Because Dwight recognized Eustace Jakes and Bob War-ner. Hard to mistake those two, even from this distance. They're town councilmen and I'd take a bet they rounded up the other six to hold a meet-ing of their own. They're all businessmen with premises on prime pieces of Sun City real estate. Always have been in favor of Carter's plans for the town. I suppose now they think they can give his scheme official backing without fear of being kicked off the council at the next election."

There was defeat in her voice and in her attitude as she leaned wearily against one of the yuccas.

"Hell, Miss Helen!" Dwight growled. "We can't just give up. We've got the press ready to print and now we have the paper to print on. Let's get down to the Black Hole and make it so people'll know our side of the story."

She sighed, unmoved by his eager optimism. "Sure, Dwight," she muttered. "Why not? It's what Harry wants. And with only two guns against so many, it's the only course open to us."

"Black Hole?" Grace asked.

"It's what the cave on the beach has always been called by local people," Helen told him. And showed a wan smile. "Not a very romantic name for a place where lots of couples first started their courting."

"The hell with romance, lady," Grace growled. "It's some hate we want to stir up down there tonight."

"God, how can people be so foolish?" the woman groaned and as she raised her gaze from her hands she found herself looking into the dark, impassive eyes of the Virginian.

He shook his head. "Right now you're asking the wrong feller, ma'am."

CHAPTER TEN

The Black Hole was cut by ancient forces into the base of the towering cliff below the grazing land of the recently killed Carl Parton. It was easy for the group to reach the cave without being seen from Sun City, for the hill, then orange groves and finally the cliff screened their curving path from the small wood.

As they moved along the beach, all on foot with the horses being led, the Pacific surf beat the shore on their right and the dark face of the rocky cliff towered above them on the left. Although this stretch of the beach was not familiar to them, Steele and Grace were able to spot the position of the cave before they saw the dark entrance which gave it its name. For a buggy with a horse still in the shafts was parked under an overhang of rock.

"How'd you get a wagon outta town without anyone knowin', lady?" Grace asked.

"It was the only way to move the equipment," Helen answered, still depressed. "We had some luck, I suppose. Maybe the last we're ever going to get."

"Everyone has the same amount of luck," Steele put in. "It's how they use it makes it good or bad."

The group fell silent again as they got closer to the buggy, Steele and Grace becoming overtly cautious—the older man draping a hand over his Remington. Their eyes shifted constantly, paying particular attention to the sand. But it was dry, fine and soft under the cliff, never touched by the ocean. Even as they lifted their own feet a million grains tumbled back into the impressions, almost filling them. So all that was left were indistinct depressions and ridges, like a thousand others which convolute the surface of the beach. Only the buggy wheels had left a clearly defined pattern which continued to show after many hours had elapsed.

When they reached the parked vehicle they could see why it had been necessary to leave the horse outside. For the entrance to the Black Hole beside the buggy was very low. Ten feet wide but only four feet high. No light or sound emerged from the cave opening.

The woman hurried on ahead, bent down and cupped her hands around her mouth to call inside.

"Harry? Is everything all right?"

There was a short pause before the newspaperman replied, "Yes, fine. Are they here?"

"Yes. They brought the paper."

"Good." His voice sounded as a somewhat eerie strong whisper, echoing off the walls of the cave and seemingly coming from a long way off.

"Here." Dwight said, taking the reins of the horses and hitching them to a rail at the side of the buggy seat. Then he lifted down the two stacks of paper from Steele's gelding, displaying easy strength.

The Virginian and Grace each claimed a stack off the stallion and the bulk and weight meant they had to use both hands. Each was conscious that this would leave him defenseless in face of a sudden attack.

"Grateful if you'd fetch my rifle, ma'am," Steele said as Helen stooped again to start into the cave.

She resented the delay, but then the feel of the Colt Hartford's metal and wood in her hands brought a grim smile to her lips. "I'll lead the way," she told the men. "It's black as pitch in there. Keep your heads down until I tell you. The roof's low for most of the way."

Steele had not realized he was sweating until he felt the cool air inside the cave brush his face and dry the beads of moisture on his skin. And then the aftereffects of his tense ride from San Varas made themselves felt as his stooped-over posture triggered a dull ache at the base of his spine. Once the moonlit entrance was behind them, no one could see even an inch in front of his face and they shuffled over the sand with one shoulder brushing the cool rack wall.

A dozen yards into the cliff, the cave narrowed and curved to the right.

"You can straighten up now," Helen Stewart told them and the sigh which Dexler Grace breathed revealed that he was suffering from the same kind of muscle ache as the Virginian.

A weak light showed ahead, and brightened as the higher roofed tunnel took another curve, this time to the left. Steele, who was immediately behind the woman, felt yet another almost painful stab of desire for her as her blonde hair took on a kind of halo while her upper body showed in stark, black silhouette against the light. He mouthed silent curses at himself, but this self-anger did nothing to quell the physical response of his lust.

Then the woman led him and Grace and Tuxon into the broad chamber of the cave proper where Andrews had set up his printing press. The cavern was sixty feet wide by half that distance deep. The roof was higher than the glow from a single kerosene lamp could reach. The press was against the rear wall with a frame of typesetting already on the bed. A cone of light fell on it from the lamp which stood on a ledge in the rock.

Harry Andrews sat on a carton of ink on the sandy floor, his back leaning against the side of the press. His black moustache looked very dark against the paleness of his complexion. He appeared weary, sick and afraid. Almost corpse-like except for his gray eyes which refused to remain still in their sockets.

"Come on, Harry," the woman urged without enthusiasm and a little irritably. "We've got

110

everything we need now. Let's start printing the *News* and . . ."

Steele and Grace dropped their burdens and it was the double thud of the newsprint to the ground which startled Helen into curtailing the sentence. Then she vented a strangled cry of fear as the Virginian shot out an arm to reach around her and snatch at the Colt Harford. At the same time as Grace went for his Remington.

"Don't!" Andrews shrieked, half rising to his feet.

The Virginian and the retired lawman ignored him, their eyes raking up from fresh footprints in the sand to seek out the men whose booted feet had made the marks.

"We'll kill the girl, you bastards!"

Grace had drawn his gun halfway out of the holster. Steele had fisted one gloved hand around the frame of the rifle. And then they both froze their moves, the younger man looking to his right and the older to the left.

It was Pat Gundry who had snarled the threat, as he stepped out of the shadows with a Winchester rifle leveled from the hip. There was a short, very fat and totally bald man of sixty some yards behind the glowering Carter hand.

"And I'm coverin' the Tuxon kid!" the recently appointed deputy named Hellen warned.

"Please!" Harry Andrews begged, coming completely erect and thrusting out his hands in an attitude of abject pleading.

Steele and Grace had swung their heads to see the full extent of the opposition. Just the three.

111

Gundry and Hellen with rifles. The third man unarmed.

"You'd condone murder, Mr. Jakes?" Helen Stewart asked, her tone thick with contempt.

"I believe in the law being upheld by duly appointed officers, young lady," Jakes retorted pompously, continuing to shelter behind Gundry. "In this instance, the apprehension of murderers and those who aid and abet them!"

Steele had allowed his hand to fall away from the Colt Hartford.

Grace said, "Shit!" and released his grip from the revolver butt.

Helen sighed as she made a half turn from the waist—and shot Pat Gundry.

There had appeared to be no hint of aggression in the woman's slow turn. Rather, it had seemed as if she was surrendering, her expression one of miserable defeat while her actions were apparently to show the Carter men that she intended to drop the rifle. Instead, she clicked back the hammer and squeezed the trigger.

The report sounded deafeningly loud in the rock confines of the cave, the explosion bouncing back and forth between the walls like some awesome noise out of a terrifying nightmare.

Gundry died from a stopped heart that pumped a final spurt of blood out through the hole in his chest—and gouted a great torrent from the massive wound where the bullet exited at his back. There was a look of uncomprehending surprise on his face as he staggered backward and started to fall.

112

It was the enormously fat Jakes who screamed, in high pitched horror as he threw himself to the ground, going under the deadly bullet but failing to escape the spray of blood it had erupted from Gundry's collapsing body.

"Oh, Jesus!" Hellen wailed, and perhaps fired his Winchester by accident or instinct rather than as a deliberate act. Then he shrieked, "No!" as he saw the woman stagger and collapse, to hit the ground a moment after Gundry's corpse folded over the still screaming Jakes.

"Ellie!" Andrews moaned, and lunged across the cave.

Even before the echo of Hellen's shot had ceased to sound, Grace drew and fired the Remington. His speed was as fast as it had been when he killed Doonon, even though it was not necessary in the cave. For Hellen was paralyzed by the shock of what he had done to the woman. He could only stare in horror at the welter of blood pouring from her side, dark red arterial blood that told of a fatal wound. The muzzle of the rifle had sagged toward the ground and he made no attempt to pump the action.

Grace went for the professional gunfighter's body shot, instinctively taking no chances. His bullet took Hellen in the chest, left of center, and its victim died as suddenly as Gundry, But spilled less blood, for the Remington did not have the power to drive its bullet completely through his body. So the man died on his feet and crumpled to the spot where he had been standing.

Steele had retrieved his rifle by then and began

to eject the spent shell, his dark eyes shifting between Jakes—who was trying to wriggle out from under the body of Gundry—and Andrews who was cradling the unfeeling head of his dead fiancée on his knees. He felt empty of all emotion for a stretched second, then experienced a surge of anger—a reckless rage because it had only one target. A pathetically frightened, old, unarmed fat man. The only man left within the confines of the cave who could be blamed for the death of Helen Stewart. And the Virginian might have killed Jakes if Dwight Tuxon had not broken the harsh, tense silence.

"Is Miss Helen dead, Mr. Andrews?"

The newspaperman looked up and wiped the tears of grief from his eyes with the back of a hand before replying," Yes, son. She's gone."

Then Andrews was gripped by rage. A more mindless and volatile brand than the one affecting Steele.

The Virginian saw this and was able to lunge forward and get between Andrews and Jakes just before the fat man got to his feet and the newspaperman made to power at him with clawed hands.

"Know just how you feel, feller," Steele murmured, holding the rifle across the front of his chest, two handed, as a bar on a level with the crouching Andrews' throat. "But it won't bring her back."

"Trite, but true," Dexler Grace added. "Anyway, there's a bigger bastard than him to kill. One way or another. Save it, Andrews."

114

"It wasn't supposed to be like this!" Jakes wailed tremulously. "I told them not to harm the innocent. But Miss Stewart . . . She fired the first . . ."

"Shut up, you sonofabitch!" Andrews snarled. "Just shut your damn mouth for a while. If you don't, I'm not sure I can . . ."

He got to his feet, whirled away from Steele and walked stiff-legged to the press. Where he leaned forward, hands hooked over the frame of typesetting and head hung low between his arms. Another tense silence filled the cave—until Andrews' body shook. He gasped, and retched to direct a great splash of evil-smelling vomit at the ground between his feet.

"Oh, my God," Jakes gasped. "I think I'm going to do that. It wasn't supposed to happen like this!"

Steele canted the Colt Hartford to his shoulder and turned slowly to gaze coldly into the sweat-sheened, trembling face of the fat man. Jakes saw the evil in the dark eyes of the Virginian and took a backward step with a strangled cry of alarm trickling over his quaking lower lip. Then his heels thudded into the blood-stained corpse of Gundry and the cry became a scream of horror as he fell across the body and rolled frantically clear.

"No, feller," Steele said, his voice as bleak as his gaze. "If you've got any guts, you're going to spill them a different way."

CHAPTER ELEVEN

"I had this idea about the Black Hole," Eustace Jakes said anxiously, his small round, yellowish eyes darting nervously around the faces of the three men and a boy who watched him. "I knew Andrews here wouldn't just up and run away after all the effort he's put in to opposing Franklin Carter. And it seemed to me that this cave was the perfect place for you people to print the *News* in secret.

"So I went to Jack Boxer's office, but he wasn't there. Just Gundry and Bill Hellen. I wanted them to get the sheriff and some more men, but they said they wanted to check out the cave first."

"On account of they're greedy, like you," Grace growled. "Carter's posted a reward for Steele and me. Payable to the man or men who bring us in. A two way split means more money than if the whole damn town gets a share."

The three corpses had been taken into the shadows. The remains of Gundry and Hellen had been dragged unceremoniously to one side of the cave while Andrews had gently carried the body of the woman to the other side. He had covered her head and shoulders with his rumpled jacket. No one had made any attempt to dignify the corpses of the two men. The newspaperman had kicked sand over his own vomit and then had joined Steele, Grace and the boy who stood in an arc around the spot where Jakes cowered on the ground.

The Virginian's one word order of "Talk," had been sufficient to draw the fast spoken explanation from the fat man.

"We saw the wagon tracks and then the wagon," the town councilman went on, spittle running out of the corners of his mouth and trickling down over his series of chins to stain his shirt collar. "And I guess I was as eager as the other two to handle it on our own by then. Andrews knows what happened next. We came in the cave and arrested him."

"He tell you he was expectin' company?" Grace asked sourly, and drew a scowl from the newspaperman.

"No," Jakes replied quickly. "Gundry was just about to try getting him to talk when Miss Stewart called from outside. Then Gundry warned Andrews that the woman would be the first to die if he didn't remain quiet. I didn't have anything to do with all that, did I, Andrews?"

"You didn't do anything or say anything," the newspaperman confirmed, his tone of voice making it an accusation.

"But you're saying a great deal now, feller," Steele pointed out. "Hope you can keep it up."

"About what?" Jakes asked, licking the saliva of fear off his lower lip.

"The council meeting after Carter and his men came to town," Andrews answered. "What decisions were taken?"

"There's no secret about that," the fat man came back. "It was agreed unanimously that we should back Franklin Carter's plans for Sun City. That will be our prime platform during the coming election campaign. So if we are re-elected Mr. Carter can feel confident that the majority of the voters are also behind him. Which will in turn encourage the investment we need to make Sun City the greatest metropolis on the West Coast."

Jakes was drawing confidence from talking and from the attentiveness of his audience. To such an extent that he seemed to forget for a while exactly where he was and to sound like a man making a political speech.

"How are you going to get around accusations of vested interest influencing your decision, Jakes?" Andrews asked. And he sounded like a cynical journalist putting a loaded question to such a politician.

"Everyone who owns property in Sun City or the surrounding area that is to be developed will have a vested interest," the councilman responded and there was a glint of triumph in his small, flesh-squeezed eyes. "And we have assurances from Franklin Carter that the present citizens of the existing town will have first offer of the parcels of land to be sold."

"All those parcels now owned by Carter or you and the other members of the council," Andrews growled, not making it a question. "The price of them sure to sky-rocket beyond the means of local people when the men with the big money move in."

Eustace Jakes was not floored by the statement. He even smiled as he said, "Mr. Carter intends to establish a bank which will extend loans to any *bona fide* purchaser of land who provides proof that he will build upon it."

Dexler Grace spat, hitting a spot in the sand midway between his own boots and the folded legs of Jakes.

"The bastard's up to the same kinda tricks he pulled in Carterville!"

"Carterville?" Andrews asked.

Grace grimaced. "Forget it, mister. You ain't got enough paper here to tell half that story. Anyway, it ain't none of your business. The same as what that sonofabitch plans for this town ain't none of mine. And I've had enough of scratchin' around like a guy that don't know what he wants to do. So happens I know exactly what I want to do. And I'm gonna do it."

He spun on his heels and strode toward the cave's exit tunnel. But came to an abrupt halt when Andrews snapped:

"Stop him, Steele!"

The retired lawman with a tarnished badge behind his coat lapel was rigid with tension—his spine ramrod stiff and contoured by his clothes, his right hand half clawed for a fast draw.

"I have to turn around, dude," he admitted. "Figure you're already lookin' at me. You could make it."

The Virginian had moved just his head to watch the older man retreat from the group at the center of the cave, the Colt Hartford still sloped to his shoulder. "I could make it, feller," he drawled. "If it was that important."

Now Grace turned his head, setting the dangling corks to swinging across his sardonically grinning face. "We ain't buddies, but we ain't enemies, right?"

"I've killed both. When it was necessary."

The old man nodded. "You know it's been the same with me, Steele. It's on account of killin' her I have to kill him. I'll see you around, maybe."

Then he left, moving out of the pool of light from the lamp. Soon after the darkness of the tunnel swallowed him, the crunch of his footfalls on the sand faded.

"Damnit, we have to disassociate ourselves from him!" Andrews snarled, swinging around angrily and striding to the press. He stood there for a moment, staring down at the made-up frames of typesetting, as if his mind had gone blank and he could not decide how to approach his new problem. "God, there's so little time!"

"Mr. Andrews?" Dwight Tuxon said anxiously.

"What is it, son?"

"Shouldn't one of us warn Carter that Grace is tryin' to kill him?"

"That's exactly what should be done," Jakes agreed, struggling to his feet. "I'm sure Franklin Carter will be sympathetically disposed to you people if you prove your good intentions by denouncing . . ."

"Carter already knows Grace is gunning for him," Steele cut in.

"Don't listen to him, Andrews," Jakes argued, backing away from the Virginian. "He's of the same violent breed as the other one. Your way is best. Give the people of Sun City the facts and let them decide. Killing proves nothing worthwhile in the end."

Steele allowed the rifle to arc slowly down from his shoulder and as the barrel was gripped by his right hand he clicked back the hammer with his left thumb. Eustace Jakes stared fixedly at the muzzle trained on his belly and came to an abrupt halt.

"No!" he rasped.

Andrews swung around and his pale face showed almost the same degree of fear as the fleshy features of the fat man.

"Just be quiet and listen," the Virginian said softly and directed a hard-eyed glance at Andrews before the newspaperman could voice a protest. "What I'm going to tell you is hearsay, but Dexler Grace had no reason to lie. Up to you whether you print it or not."

He glanced again at Andrews and saw he had captured the man's interest.

"I'd rather hear it direct from Grace."

"He wouldn't tell it to you, feller. Shows him up in the same bad light as Carter. Maybe worse."

"You don't have to point that rifle at me, mister," Jakes whined. "Why are you doing that to me?"

"I've been having a bad time, fat man," Steele hissed between clenched teeth. "And I may have to kill someone to relieve my feelings. Just want to be sure that if I can't think straight, my aim is."

"You're crazy!" the councilman accused, fear driving his voice to a high pitch. "Clear out of your mind!"

"Keep talking, feller," the Virginian urged, his teeth still pressed together between his lips that were curled hard back.

"What?"

"It would be a great relief to me if you talked yourself to death."

CHAPTER TWELVE

Steele rode south along the beach, his weathered face wearing a frown of dissatisfaction in the pale moonlight of the pre-dawn hour. The night air was at its coolest, a gentle breeze off the ocean pressing tendrils of moist, salt-tasting mist against him.

He had told Harry Andrews everything he knew about Carterville in its heyday, the newspaperman's interest becoming more avid by the moment. Often, the obese Eustace Jakes had been on the point of ignoring the rifle's threat to voice his rejection of what the Virginian was saying. But always the lamp-lit, killer glint in the dark eyes of Steel had driven the man back into grimacing silence.

Not until he had completed the catalogue of Carter's crimes did he reveal the part Grace had played. And this was the reason for his discontent as he rode far south of Sun City before turning inland and then swinging north. For he felt he had betrayed a man who had done him no wrong and for a reason that was not founded upon self-interest.

If he had stood to gain from giving the story credence by revealing Grace to be corrupt and a multiple murderer, he could have understood his motives. But he had nothing to either win or lose, whatever the outcome of events in Sun City. At least, nothing he could fathom no matter how deeply he delved into his mind. Which was why he felt compelled to return to the town instead of heading away from it: certain of only one thing. That he would never be able to rest easy unless he could disprove Jakes' taunt: *"You're crazy!"* For, in retrospect, almost everything he had done since arriving in Sun City was triggered by impulse. Which, for a man like Steele destined to walk the thin line between life and death, added up to sheer madness.

The sea mist which began to break up on the broad beach was almost completely dissipitated by the time it had curled over the high ground and rolled down into town. And he had a clearer view of Sun City now than when he had first seen it, yesterday morning, shrouded with heat haze. For, as the moon got paler, so the first light of a new dawn strengthened its hold on the eastern sky.

Nothing moved on the two streets and there was no light, smoke or sound from any of the buildings which flanked them. The scent of growing citrus fruit was just beginning to make inroads into the salty tang of the atmosphere.

He made his survey of the silent town from behind a rock on the crest of the slope which had been his first vantage point. His gelding was hitched in a small stand of timber on the southern side of the rise, hidden from the direction of Sun City and protected by leafy trees should Steele's business in town hold him throughout the heat of the new day.

The ready cocked Colt Hartford in a double-handed grip, he made his way down the slope zig-zagging to make use of scattered boulders and infrequent hollows to the west of the trail. He had been within effective rifle range from the moment he reached the crest of the rise. So he gave free rein to his sixth sense for being watched while carefully using his eyes and ears as he headed for the back lot of the first house on the west side of south Main Street. He neither saw nor heard anything to warn him of danger and yet he could not shake off a suspicion that his progress was under surveillance.

He could not pinpoint the position of the eyes he felt sure were watching him and as he reached the cover of a shack out back of the house, he fastened upon a logical reason for this. Dexler Grace was back in Sun City and the early morning silence clamped over the town meant he had not yet accomplished his aim in being there. So perhaps he was having second thoughts: had decided in the cool light of breaking day to give Harry Andrews a final chance to do things his way. In which event he would be waiting and watching, from a position where he would miss nothing of any importance—like a dudishly dressed man with a rifle moving furtively into town.

Or, Steele was prepared to admit as he worked his way across the back lots of the Main Street buildings, it was his imagination playing tricks on him. It had done so before, in similar situations of danger and tension when his subconscious was influenced by the confusion affecting his mind. And his mind was certainly not clear now: had not been since he saw Helen Stewart die, prevented Andrews attacking Eustace Jakes only to threaten the helpless fat man himself.

As he reached the alley at the side of the sheriff's office he shook his head and mouthed a tacit curse, angry at himself. The past and his contributions to it were unimportant. He had survived and he had a plan of action. It was vital now to think clearly with a mind uncluttered by the side issues of why he was acting as he was.

He reached the end of the alley and carefully checked the whole length of Pacific Street. It was as deserted and devoid of lights as Main. He set his feet down lightly on the strip of raised sidewalk in front of the sheriff's office and breathed a silent sigh of satisfaction when he discovered the door unlocked. Light from outside—stronger now from the dawning day than the failing moon—penetrated the single window and the glass panel in the door to reveal the layout of the office.

An uncluttered desk with a chair in back and in front of it. A large safe. A rack of six Winchester rifles. A barred door in a side wall which gave

126

on to a short hallway leading to three cells. The cells were empty. The office smelled of stale cigar smoke.

Steele vented another low sigh of satisfaction as he sank gratefully into the padded chair behind the desk, resting the barrel of the Colt Hartford on the desk top, aimed at the door. So far he had called it right. Gundry and Hellen had been detailed to remain on duty all night and everyone else in town was bedded down when Jakes got his idea about the Black Hole and came to the office. The three men had left Sun City without disturbing anyone else.

But soon the rising sun would begin to rouse people and, if things continued to go Steele's way, Jack Boxer would come to his office to check with his deputies. Alone would be perfect, but the Virginian had had plenty of experience of dealing with the imperfect.

The gray of morning brightened, then lost the dingy color of first light as the leading arc of the sun broke clear of the eastern horizon. The sounds of opening doors and window shutters began to disturb the tranquility of the town. Then the aroma of woodsmoke permeated the warming air that crept into the office through the crack at the foot of the door. Steele felt hungry, ran the back of a gloved hand across the bristles of his jaw and felt dirty.

Men in work clothes walked or rode past the law office and if any of them glanced in through the window they failed to recognize the man sitting at the desk.

Sheriff Jack Boxer pushed open the door an hour after Steele had claimed his chair and did not realize anything was wrong until he had put one foot over the threshold.

"I don't want to kill you, feller," the Virginian said evenly. "But lots of people have to do lots of things they don't want to. Come in and close the door."

The lawman had come to an abrupt halt, shock deeply inscribed into the flesh of his florid face. He saw the threat of the aimed rifle before he could move his hand a fraction of an inch toward his holstered revolver.

"Where's Pat Gundry and . . ."

"Step inside and sit down," Steele cut in. "And close the door behind you."

Shock was replaced by anger in Boxer's narrow blue eyes. He shook his head, but it was not a refusal to comply with the orders. He carried them out silently, careful to keep his hand far away from his gun. Just before he could voice another question, Steele spoke.

"They're more work for the undertaker, Sheriff. In a cave on the beach called the Black Hole. You know it?"

Boxer's anger expanded and he swallowed hard, as if the emotion was something tangible that threatened to spew from his mouth and get him killed. "I know it," he said hoarsely. "You killed them?"

"No."

"Grace?"

"He killed the one who killed Helen Stewart."

128

Steele watched the lawman's face take on and lose a series of expressions. Disbelief, shock, anger again, confusion.

"Came here because I don't reckon you're the worst sheriff in California, feller," the Virginian said. "But that would never have been a good enough reason if the woman hadn't died the way she did. You were carrying a torch for her, weren't you?"

"How'd it happen?" His voice was croakier than ever.

"I said you were carrying a torch for her?"

"Damnit, I aimed to put a ring on her finger before Andrews showed up!"

Steele nodded, calm in face of his rage. A rage that was brought under control rather than diminished as the lawman listened to the Virginian's account of the night's events—from the time he and Grace left Sun City for San Varas until Boxer opened his office door. During this period, listening to the even-toned drawl, grief began to exert its influence on the sheriff. So that there was a catch in his throat when he spoke, robbing his tone of resolution.

"Way you tell it, Helen killed a deputy in the execution of his duty. The other deputy had to shoot her in self defense."

"If you're really convinced of that, feller," Steele said softly, "then I'm going to have to kill you as my first move to get out of this town. Because it means you're as committed to Franklin Carter as the men he pays. Or maybe he does pay you."

129

Anger flared in his blue eyes, then died as suddenly as it had ignited. "He tried, mister. I wanted no part of that. So he gave me Rich Doonon instead. It was working out fine."

"Until it turned sour."

"The crowd you tied in with stirred the crap, mister," Boxer defended heatedly. "I ain't ever had any reason to figure Carter as anything but a benefactor for Sun City. And now all I've got is some story told by a driftin' gunslinger with reason to hate the man." He paused, then nodded. "And even if all Grace said about the town up north is true, that don't have to mean Franklin Carter figures to do the same thing again here."

"Up to you, Sheriff," Steele responded, getting up from the chair and swinging the Colt Hartford slowly to cant it to his left shoulder. "This isn't my town. I've got no stake in it. Been the easiest thing in the world for me to ride away instead of coming back in."

"So why didn't you, mister?" Boxer snarled, but there was no anger in his eyes. They were filled with confusion.

"Not because I care about Sun City, feller. Last night I killed a man named Regan. I'd like to be sure something good comes out of it. That I won't be wanted for murder."

"And you figure that gettin' off the hook is as easy as comin' in here and just talkin'?"

"No, feller. I reckon it's a matter of letting the people decide after they've read what Andrews is printing in his newspaper."

Boxer scowled. "But you ain't about to let me lock you up until that decision's made, I guess?"

Steele showed his boyish grin as he looked down across the desk at the seated lawman. "Reckon I'm already in a trap, feller. Walked into it of my own account. Don't intend to spring it closed myself."

"So what do you intend, mister?"

"To let you get up and walk out of this office, Sheriff. Andrews is printing his newspaper in secret but he's going to have to come out into the open to get it to his readers. I reckon no one will read it with more interest than Carter. What Carter does then is anybody's guess. You're the law in Sun City so if what he does is against the law . . ."

Steele allowed the sentence to hang unfinished in the rapidly warming air.

"You're a real cool customer, mister," Boxer growled.

"Who happens to believe the law in Sun City isn't for sale," the Virginian replied. "If that's wrong, you'll be the one who pays. With your life."

CHAPTER THIRTEEN

The sheriff left the office first, stepping out onto the sun bright Pacific Street with the deep lines of a frown cut into his face. The farmers and growers who rose early to start their day's work were already out in the fields and groves and the street was empty again. For the stores were not yet open and the women who would patronize them were engaged in preparing breakfast or clearing up after the meal.

"It's okay," Boxer growled. "Looks to be, anyway. I can't be sure of nothin' anymore."

"Don't they say the only sure thing in life is death?" Steele countered.

The lawman vented a grunt of disgust and swung right, to head along the sidewalk toward the intersection. The Virginian stepped outside and turned in the other direction, then into the alley, where he leaned against the side of the office building and waited. He did not trust Boxer and knew the sheriff did not trust him. But he was certain that he had made a correct judgment of the man.

Jack Boxer was a man of the law as well as a lawman. As such, he could be deeply affected by the death of a woman he had loved but would not allow this to influence him in carrying out his duty. What Helen Stewart's violent end and Steele's appearance in his office had done was to trigger him out of his complacent attitude toward Franklin Carter.

But there would be doubt in the man's mind as he walked down the street to the intersection and across to the Sun City Hotel where Carter and his men had spent the night. And it could happen that the rancher with questionable plans for the town might be able to talk away Boxer's doubt. Which would close the trap on Steele as surely as if he had agreed to be locked in one of the cells.

He chanced to look out of the alley mouth and along Pacific Street, in time to see Boxer step down off the sidewalk and angle across the intersection toward the entrance to the hotel. The lawman reached the center of the crossroads when something caused him to halt and turn his head to look northward along Main Street. Because of the buildings which intervened, it took a few seconds more for the thud of galloping hooves to reach Steele's ears. Then a movement on the periphery of his vision caused the Virginian to shift his gaze away from Boxer and look at the roofline of the hotel: a part of a second before a man ducked out of sight behind the sign atop the two-storey building. The tell-tale corks dangling from the brim of the man's hat revealed who it was hiding up there.

133

The cadence of the hoofbeats was reduced as the riders slowed their mounts, so that the hard-breathing horses raised very little dust as they were reined to a halt on the intersection: a close knit group of a half dozen.

The only man Steele recognized was the squat, gray-haired Ed Logan, the editor of the *San Varas Journal*, who wore a bandage instead of a hat on his head. The other five were younger, tougher looking men wearing gunbelts and carrying rifles in their boots. The one who swung down from his saddle and shook Boxer's hand had a sun-glinting badge pinned to a pocket of his shirt. The exchange of words between the two men was brief, ended by a gesture from the Sun City lawman that they should continue their talk in the hotel. The rest of the riders dismounted and led their horses to where they hitched them before trailing Boxer into the lobby.

Steele glanced up at the hotel's roof sign again and showed a brief, tight smile as a hand was raised in greeting or simply to confirm that Dexler Grace had spotted his erstwhile partner and knew the sighting had been mutual.

The arrival of the posse from San Varas was something the Virginian had not counted on and he had to regard it as a bad sign unless events proved otherwise. So he changed his vantage point, certain Grace saw him but unable to tell if other eyes watched him.

He simply stepped out of the alley and strolled with surface nonchalance across Pacific Street, taking the straightest line as the shortest distance between two points, then treading lightly on the sidewalk across the front of two stores to reach the mouth of an alley on the north side of the street.

A thin, fraught looking woman was hanging out laundry on a length of line in back of her house and he had to wait until she had returned indoors before making his cautious way to the rear of the Luck Lady Saloon. Store shacks, a wagon and heaps of discarded household items provided infrequent cover from the rear windows of the buildings. A dog barked at him once, but the animal was on a short chain and sank back into sulking silence when a young boy's voice shouted at him to be quiet.

Small sounds came from inside a back room of the saloon: the hiss of a steaming pot on a stove, the rattle of crockery and the curses of a man preparing breakfast and not enjoying the chore.

Standing at the rear door of the building, the predominant odor to reach Steele's nostrils was from the privy across the yard: a stench which totally masked the scents of the ocean, the fruit groves and woodsmoke. But then his tastebuds swelled as he caught the aroma of fresh made coffee. On the other side of the door the man curtailed his curses to sigh and smack his lips.

The Virginian pursed his own lips, drew in a deep breath and pushed open the door, thrusting the barrel of the rifle into the gap.

"Good morning, Lester," he greeted the toothless, watery-eyed bartender. "You got a cup of that brew to spare?"

The old man, clad in a filthy nightshirt, was seated at a greasy table in the greasy kitchen, a cup of coffee held in both hands to his slack mouth. His eyes bulged and he made a gagging sound as Steele stepped over the threshold. Then, as the door closed behind the intruder, Lester began to tremble. So violently that the cup slipped from his hands, hit the edge of the table and spilled boiling hot coffee into his lap. But fear was too powerful to allow him to feel the pain of being scalded.

Steele felt a stab of self-contempt as he sloped the rifle to his shoulder and approached the stove. Twice within a few hours he had struck terror into the hearts of helpless old-timers. While he had left it, with one exception, up to another not so helpless old man to take care of the dangerous enemies.

"Take it easy," he soothed as he poured himself a cup of coffee and carried it to the table, where he sat down opposite Lester. "It's just that I have some time to spare."

Lester began to experience the searing pain of the hot coffee now and he grimaced as he massaged his thighs and groin. "Why here?"

"It seems the in-place has changed to the Sun City Hotel, feller. And I don't reckon they'd welcome an outsider like me." He sipped the coffee and showed a grimace of his own. "How many times have you used these grounds?"

"I wasn't expectin' company, Steele. You don't have to drink it, you don't like it."

"It's wet."

"And friggin' hot!" the old man countered, fully recovered from shock. "You gotta be crazy comin' back to this town, large as life."

A nod. "You're not the first to think so, feller. And I'm not so sure you and the rest aren't right to . . ."

He broke off and cocked his head, listening hard to identify a sound. When Lester seemed about to question him, he held up a gloved hand. The sound swelled, and became combined with others. Hoofbeats, and the turning wheels and creaking timbers of a wagon. Heading in off the north trail onto Main Street. The horse hauling the wagon was trotting. More hoofbeats sounded and men shouted.

"What's happenin'?" Lester asked nervously.

But Steele was already on his feet and making for the door which gave on to the saloon.

"Hey, is it all right for me to come take a look?" the old-timer called.

"If you want," the Virginian allowed, jerking open the door and staring across the saloon. "But keep your head down."

"What?" Lester called from the kitchen doorway as Steele slid the bolt on two doors which barred the batwinged entrance of the Lucky Lady.

"Could be more than the *Sun City News* that's about to hit the streets, feller."

CHAPTER FOURTEEN

"EXTRA EDITION, extra edition!" Dwight Tuxon yelled above the noise and through the billowing dust. "*Sun City News*! Read the truth about Franklin Carter's plans for your town!"

The boy with a plague of boils marring his good looks was standing on the rear of the buggy, legs splayed to brace himself on the fast moving vehicle as he used both hands to scatter copies of the newspaper over each side.

The rangy Harry Andrews was in the seat, pale faced but with his jaw and mouthline in a more determined set than ever. He had no difficulty in maintaining his position, for he was firmly wedged between the corpses of Helen Stewart on one side of him and Pat Grundy and Hellen on the other. The bodies were securely lashed to the seat.

The buggy careened past the Lucky Lady just as Steele thrust open the doors. Behind it were men on horseback and on foot, some of them attempting to read the newspapers they had scooped up from the dusty ground. They were the men who had left town early to start work in the fields and citrus groves. Their number swollen by other men and some women who had been brought from their houses by the commotion and then paused only long enough to grab at the scattered newspapers.

The printed words, Tuxon's excited shouts and the sight of the three swaying corpses aboard the buggy held the shocked attention of everyone who ran onto the street. And nobody took any notice of the Virginian in the saloon doorway until the sweating and breathless Eustace Jakes came waddling by, purple-faced from the exertion of having to trail the buggy on foot all the way from the Black Hole. He was close to exhaustion and dropping further behind the buggy and its noisily excited entourage with every step.

Perhaps he could have continued to run all the way to the intersection before he collapsed, but when he glimpsed the familiar rifle-toting figure of Adam Steele he came to an abrupt halt, rocked back and forth for a few moments, then crumpled as his legs gave way beneath him.

"This is madness!" he managed to force out between gasps for breath.

"Reckon it is at your age," Steele answered, stepping out of the saloon and swinging right to head down Main Street.

"Get me a drink, Lester," Jakes croaked.

"Get it yourself!" the nightshirted bartender snapped, falling in behind the Virginian and, like him, stooping to snatch up a copy of the *Sun City News*.

Steele glanced at the large type headlines: WE DON'T WANT CARTER CORRUPTION HERE . . . LOCAL WOMAN MURDERED BY CARTER MAN . . . WHY DID DOONON KILL PARTON? . . . FORMER LAWMAN TELLS ALL ABOUT CARTERVILLE . . . HOW THE "NEWS" CAME TO YOU TODAY.

He didn't need to read the stories under the headlines since he had either heard them already or been a part of them as they happened. So he tossed the newspaper aside and concentrated his attention on the intersection at the center of town, sparing several glances up at the roof of the Sun City Hotel.

Dexler Grace was out of sight but seemed to be the only person in town who chose to remain so. Andrews had halted the buggy outside the hotel and was sitting calmly on the seat. Behind him, Dwight Tuxon continued to stand and distribute copies of the newspaper, but he was no longer shouting. And the crowd which gathered on the intersection also quietened as each individual acquired a *Sun City News* and scanned its contents. But few read far into the stories before their attention was drawn back to the bullet-shattered corpses tied in place to either side of the silent Andrews.

If anybody noted Steele's approach toward the rear of the tightly packed crowd it did not cause even a ripple of interest. Then what little talk still continued was abruptly curtailed by the opening of the glass paneled doors of the hotel.

A copy of the newspaper had been taken inside, for the man who emerged held it in both hands. He was a man past seventy, not quite so tall as he used to be because age had stooped his shoulders and put a curve in his back. He was freshly shaved and groomed, dressed in a well-cut tailored suit with a cravat between the wide lapels of his jacket. He was hatless to show a full head of silver gray hair above a thin, tanned, angular featured face. His slender frame looked pathetically weak while in his face could be seen an unmistakable strength of character.

He came to a halt on the edge of the sidewalk and shook his head sadly as his bright blue eyes completed a cursory survey of the silent crowd. Then he began to read the front page of the newspaper, his expression unchanged. He was not disturbed by sounds from behind him: of the doors opening and Sheriff Boxer stepping outside and of second storey windows being pushed up by hard-eyed men who immediately got their hands out of sight.

Then silence again, which seemed somehow to emphasize the building heat of the rising sun. The hot seconds ticked away. Everyone except Steele stared fixedly at Franklin Carter as he read the newspaper. The Virginian divided his attention between Boxer, the men at the windows and the unmoving roofline of the hotel. His mind was disturbed by a nagging worry that the posse from San Varas were nowhere to be seen.

Once, his gaze found and locked on that of Jack Boxer, but the Sun City lawman merely tightened his mouthline in a gesture that was meaningless. It was obvious that the Carter men at the hotel windows were armed but, as far as Steele was able to see, among the people on the intersection, only he and the sheriff had guns.

"You're a good writer, Mr. Andrews," Carter said suddenly, his voice sounding more powerful than it was in the tense silence. "But I think you should forget about journalism and get into dime novels."

As he finished speaking he opened his hands to allow the newspaper to float down through the hot air to settle in the dust of the street.

"Seems to me, Mr. Carter," Andrews replied, and there was a nervous catch in his voice, "that it is up to the people of Sun City to decide on that."

The rancher sucked his teeth. "What do you suggest. A head count, maybe? "He held up a hand and began to touch his fingers. "Doonon. Regan. Holcombe. Hellen. Gundry. That's five dead on my side. Carl Parton and Miss Stewart, Two for you. Or is there another way you want to score it?"

"I notice you didn't count what was left of Bart Dixon after he blew up the *News* office," Andrews retorted. "Or doesn't he rate?"

"He rates, you sonofabitch!" one of the men at the window called down. "He was my best buddy."

"Shut your mouth, Cal!" Carter snapped, allowing his composure to slip for a moment.

But Dixon's friend had opened a breach which allowed others to contribute to the dangerous discussion.

"We haven't heard you deny what it says in the paper, Mr. Carter?" somebody called from the center of the crowd.

There was a murmuring of agreement with this, which lengthened the time it took the rancher to recover from the first interruption.

"If it was worthy of denial I would do just that! But I do not intend to give such a scandal sheet whatever dignity it might draw from a denial. What I do intend is to build a city on this site. A great and proud city from which anyone with courage and imagination will profit a whole lot. And if there were not ladies present, I would spit on this lie-packed newspaper. As I would wish to spit on everyone and everything that stands in the way of progress."

He had regained control of himself, but now as he warmed to his subject he began to sweat and his voice wavered.

"Last night your elected councilmen voted to back my scheme for Sun City. They have had their doubts before, as you all know. But they are finally convinced that my plans are in the best interests of this town and the people who live here. My only regret is that my opponents had to resort to violence—to murder good and honest men— in order for me to get the backing I sought to obtain by peaceful and democratic means.

143

"Count the dead, you people. And read the printed lies if you must. But remember that Parton and Miss Stewart were killed by duly appointed sheriff's deputies. Whereas my men were murdered by professional killers hired by those opposed to me."

Carter stepped down off the sidewalk and the crowd between the hotel and the stalled buggy split into two so that he could approach where Harry Andrews sat on the seat between the corpses. There had been no vocal response as he concluded his argument, but a smile began to play along his mouthline as he moved out of the shade of the sidewalk awning and into the bright sunlight. He looked a lot older in the glare, but perhaps it was due to the slow, painful way he walked.

He halted six feet from the buggy and his expression altered to one of scorn as he fastened his triumphant gaze on the pale face of Harry Andrews. "Please accept my condolences upon the tragic death of Miss Stewart," he said without altering the lines of his face. "But I believe it was she rather than you who advocated the use of violence to gain . . ."

The question of who was the faster—Dexler Grace with the Remington or Steele with the Colt Hartford—was never answered.

The Virginian saw Grace appear at the side of the hotel sign and draw his revolver. Heard the man's shout of: "Carter!"

The rifle did not have to arc away from the

shoulder very far to draw a bead on the highly placed target. But the movement was positive enough to catch the attention of several men watching from the windows. Nervously confused men who had also heard the name of their boss yelled from above them.

Revolver and rifle barrels were thrust across window ledges and the men crouched behind the guns.

Some women screamed and a few men cursed. Hands trembled, feet shuffled and eyes switched back and forth in their sockets. There was a stink of panic—or perhaps just body odor—in the hot morning air.

Franklin Carter swung around and squinted up at Grace.

Sheriff Boxer reached for his holstered Colt and took a step forward, desperate to get out from under the sidewalk awning to where he could see what everyone else was looking at.

All this in a fleeting moment of time. During which Steele knew he might be able to save the life of Carter, but only in exchange for his own. For the men at the windows—or perhaps just one man—would certainly mistake his intention.

He sloped the rifle back to his shoulder.

Grace, a grin of triumph visible through the dangling corks, squeezed the trigger of the Remington. An awkward, downward shot fired from the hip at the end of a fast draw. Perhaps off target or perhaps not. For maybe he intended a head shot—aimed to place the bullet through

Carter's clenched teeth, still displayed in the sneer of contempt which had been directed at Harry Andrews.

The gunshot exploded panic in the crowd: a pandemonium of movement and sound which suddenly quickened in tempo and rose in pitch as shock-widened eyes saw blood spurt from the head of the crumpling Franklin Carter.

Steele was caught in the human tide as people whirled and lunged forward, desperate to escape from the threat of the gunman on the roof of the Sun City Hotel. He tried to turn, but failed. Was carried backward for several feet, then fell hard to the ground. He held onto his rifle and covered his face with his forearms as people raced around and over him.

Another gunshot sounded, and signaled a fusilade.

He was in the clear, bruised and battered in a cloud of settling dust. He struggled to his feet, blinking against the muzzle flashes of fired rifles which lanced out of the hotel windows.

But nobody died, the bullets cracking high into the air across the roofs on the other side of the intersection.

Voices snapped orders in the rooms behind the open windows. The Carter men swung their heads. More terse words were spoken, indistinct through the noise outside as the citizens of Sun City scrambled into the cover of surrounding buildings. Which left three men and a boy in the dangerous open. Andrews and Tuxon aboard the buggy, Steele twenty feet behind it and Boxer midway between it and the hotel entrance. Then Dexler Grace stepped clear of the sign on the roof. As the Carter men loosened grips on their guns. Some thudded to the floor in the rooms. Others bounced from the window sills, to the sidewalk awning and then came to rest on the dusty ground.

The final impact of the last weapon to be discarded signaled another silence in the town. Broken by the husky voice of Dwight Tuxon asking, "What on earth is goin' on, Mr. Andrews?"

The newspaperman, looking pale enough to be on the edge of unconsciousness, turned his head and shook it, helpless and dumbstruck.

Sheriff Boxer did not shift his eyes or the aim of his Colt away from Grace as he provided the answer to the boy's question. "Got me some help with no axe to grind. A posse from the San Varas sheriff's office and a few Sun City people. Figured to keep the lid on things until folks got a chance to read the newspaper and make up their own minds." His tone got harsher. "I didn't count on you havin' the gall to be sittin' up there on top of a powder keg, Grace!"

More words were spoken in the hotel rooms and the men withdrew from the windows.

"He'd have won, Sheriff," Grace countered, pushing the well-used Remington into its holster. "He never did lose anythin' in all the time I knew him. Except his life."

"And I've got a whole townful of witnesses saw you take that from him, mister!" Boxer snarled. "Saw you gun down an unarmed man. There's been a lot of killin' the law'll have to deal with. No tellin' how them affairs will turn out. But you'll hang for shootin' Mr. Carter, that's for sure!"

Myron Goldstein, the bespectacled night desk clerk of the Sun City Hotel backed out of the doors and held one of them open while aiming a revolver with his other hand. The sound and movement distracted Boxer and he glanced away from Grace to see the first of a line of Carter men file into the sunlight.

"So you toss away your gun and give yourself up peace . . ."

He returned his gaze to the roof, but was an instant too late to save himself. For Grace's draw was far too fast for him, even though the Sun City lawman had his Colt out and aimed.

Steele swung the rifle away from his shoulder and this time had no reason to reverse the move. He squeezed the trigger and the Colt Hartford's report was the only one to sound. The bullet entered Grace's chest on a steep upward trajectory and burst clear of his left shoulder ahead of a great welter of crimson droplets. Perhaps it touched his heart.

The impact thudded the man hard against the hotel sign where he rested for a few stretched seconds. His gun was still in his hand, but hung low, aimed at his own foot. He worked a smile on to his time-lined face.

"Thanks, buddy," he said, his voice a rasping, pained whisper in the tense silence. "I wouldn't have made it. And this is better than the rope."

He fell forward then, his arms going out ahead of him. His hat with the dangling corks fell off and dropped to the ground. But he retained a death grip on the Remington, his fingers fisted tightly around the butt, his hand hanging over the edge of the roof.

"You figure that lets you off the hook, Steele?" Boxer growled, his voice taut with the shock of his narrow escape from death.

The Virginian cocked the hammer of the rifle as he sloped it to its familiar position against his left shoulder. He started forward, south across the intersection, heading for the gap between the sheriff and the parked buggy.

"I reckon I'm going to leave this town, feller," he answered as the Carter men continued to come out of the hotel, escorted by the grim faced San Varas posse and a half dozen anxious looking local citizens. "Or die in the attempt."

People emerged from the buildings on three sides of the intersection but did not advance more than a few paces.

"Why did you do it?" Boxer asked.

"Seemed like the right thing to do, feller."

"After a lot of the wrong ones, uh?" the lawman growled scornfully.

"Reckon a lot of people have made a lot of mistakes in this town."

Boxer sighed. "You can say that again. And your first one was stickin' around, Mister. Can't figure why you did that."

Steele was directly between the sheriff and the buggy. He halted to glance briefly up at the seat, ignoring Andrews and two of the corpses to look at the stiffening body and hung forward head of Helen Stewart. He realized it had always been impossible and discovered that he was not able to think anything of the dead woman now.

"Guess you could put it down to a passing fancy," he drawled and started toward the south stretch of Main Street again. Which put his back to Boxer and every other man in Sun City who held a gun. "Keep your badge clean, Sheriff," he added.

"I don't get you, mister!" came the growled response.

"Don't understand myself sometimes," the Virginian muttered, the words reaching only his own ears. "Just know I've been going through a bad . . .

PERIOD."*

* *But Adam Steele has not come to a full stop. He returns in the next book of this series.*